FRANC
LIFE THROUGH
FELINE EYES

FRANC
LIFE THROUGH
FELINE EYES

FABIOLA PIEDAD MARIA ALICIA REYNALES de BERRY

ISBN 978-0-9924911-2-3

Dedication

To our beloved feline Franc who inspired me to write this story

Acknowledgements

To my husband for his patience while I was writing this book

By the author

Sex and other bits-Ghosts and raw emotions

CHAPTER 1

My life began as the lives of other pussycats begin. Sometimes our fate is beyond our control, because humans are in charge, and our life depends on the good nature of the humans who receive us into their world.

I don't recall a lot about my life prior to the moment when I was taken away from mummy pussycat; myself and two of my brothers were taken to a place which had a rancid smell, there were other animals at that place, the air was heavy and somehow I felt it wasn't going to be a happy experience. I was placed in a window with my brothers and other animals, the humans said they were dogs and called them puppies, those puppies used to wee everywhere, and it was only late in the afternoon when the paper was changed. It was hot in that window, and the wee smell was overpowering to one's senses.

We all tried to sleep to forget our misery, however, from time to time our sleep was interrupted when we were passed onto a human who looked at us and checked our general appearance. The sales person talked for a long time as she tried to convince the human to buy one of us, and often mentioned that we were good value, whatever that meant.

I would've been just two or three months old, I had been in the window with the puppies for over a week, nobody cuddled us. Sometimes humans said we were cute, gave us a pat on the head and then left.

I saw a girl, not very pretty, her hair was dark and long, and she had very red lips. She entered the shop, talked to the sales woman, and both proceeded to walk towards the window where I was.

The sales woman took me out of the basket and handed me to the girl, who repeatedly said how cute I was, and what a wonderful colour my coat had.

After some deliberation she took me with her and began to walk towards the counter where the cash register was, she paid for me, and she held me in her hands as she walked out of the shop; I didn't have a chance to say good bye to my brothers. She appeared to be kind and at the same time she was very happy with her purchase, she said some words with a soft voice as she continued walking towards the place where she lived.

On the way to the place where I was going to share my life with the person who just bought me, we stopped to buy some cat food at the corner shop, she showed her purchase to the shop owner who made the comment: 'Oh, not another cat for this neighbourhood'. She smiled nervously and said that he should be grateful because there weren't many rodents in the area; said a polite goodbye to the shopkeeper and left the shop.

We finally arrived at an old, dilapidated building, when she opened the creaking, ratty, heavy timber door a dusty old smell was the first impression I had of my new place of residence. As soon as we arrived we went straight to the kitchen to find a little plate to deposit the contents of the tin, some morsels, which I ate voraciously because we didn't have much food at the shop. I had never tasted anything like that; moist, soft little chunks with a delicious meaty sauce.

All I had eaten until then was some type of hard food which was difficult to swallow.

She sat on an old metal chair with shiny legs and chipped light blue paint; she looked at me while I ate the food, and talked for a while about things I didn't understand; then began to tell me that she was thinking about the name she'd like to give me. She lifted me off the floor and sat me on her lap. Suddenly she said: I think I should call you 'Franc'. That was the name of the best boyfriend I ever had. I never asked him whether his name was short for Francis or Francisco, let's say it was short for Francisco, it sounds like a Spanish aristocrat who wore silk attire, bows on his shoes, and a hat with peacock feathers.

A man with a name like Francisco must've left his country with a trail of servants, and the idea of finding adventure and gold in the Americas; it sounds more exciting than Francis. Wasn't Francis a saint? I wonder what he did to become a saint. Maybe he flagellated his back a thousand times with a feather duster until the flesh went red with pleasure.

You ought to know, I was a real idiot to let that guy leave me, look at me, I am forty two years old, I look like a shapeless balloon, I live in a dusty rented old place, I don't even have a boyfriend. It seems very difficult to find a man these days; they are gay, are married or even worse they are divorced, bitter to the core and with an array of children to provide maintenance for. A big package to take on board and I am not a child loving person. 'The situation is grim'.

I will tell you about Franc. He was handsome to me, he had reddish hair with a bit of a wave, he didn't have any freckles as it is common in red haired people, and his complexion was quite clear of blemishes.

He had insipid, transparent blue eyes that looked as he was imploring for something all the time, and that really irritated me. Why did the colour of his eyes irritate me? I can't tell you. Perhaps it was the clarity and the transparency than made me feel uneasy about something I couldn't understand. When he looked at me through those clear eyes it was as if he put me on an x ray machine, and I felt he could see my skeleton under the garments. It gave me goose bumps.

All these thoughts existed only in my twisted mind. I was accustomed to be with guys that treated me badly after a short period of time. I have an incredible number of so called failed amorous relationships, that to count them all I need more than the fingers of my hands, I have to include all my toes, and I think I need to borrow fingers from someone else.

I always fall for the talkative one, the bullshit artist, the smart ass, the life of the party guy, the one who drinks beer standing on his head, the one who tells jokes when there isn't anything to talk about. The guy who wants to go to the pub every second day, the one who hasn't achieved much; the one who after he had his rocks off leaves you without even a look, or without saying the word thank you for allowing me to use you, and thank you that I didn't have to pay a prostitute.

Franc was kind and said he loved me, brought me flowers regularly, took me to the best restaurants fairly often and he was gentle and considerate. He liked to go for walks in the park and admired nature; unfortunately the worst part was that he liked to go to the opera, and also listened to classical music. I just couldn't stand that type of music. I am an ordinary girl.

He insisted for a while perhaps hoping that I would take some interest in it and would appreciate the beauty of those sounds as he described them.

He explained what an adagio and a sotto voce were, he knew the story of the librettos, the time when the opera was written and the composer's name; but instead of learning or at least show a desire to learn about his interest, I made fun of him and began to mock his opera singers.

I arrived at home one night, he had prepared dinner, the table was set on the balcony looking at the sea and the beach, candles on the table, a bottle of wine, and that bloody music began to flow.

He explained that it was a very beautiful baroque opera about Julius Caesar and Cleopatra. Listen to the castrato voice. Natural castrato voices are very rare. There have been some famous castrati, like Farinelli. Close your eyes and just let the music enter the pores of your skin, feel the vibration of the melody fill your soul, he instructed me.

I made fun of him and his antiquated tastes which I found suffocating. The dinner was ruined and all I did was to make him very upset after he did his best to educate me.

He also read complicated books about history; well, I thought to be complicated, and he liked to discuss those historical events with me. He often mentioned that it was truly regrettable that those subjects, in general, were presented devoid of interest to children while at school.

He also said that history was very important because the consequences of it are lived today, and tomorrow is made of today. In the same way that personal beliefs, actions, and decisions we make today, have an impact on our personal life tomorrow.

Franc often talked about ancient Greek history, the early philosophers and how their theories are relevant even today; but his very favourite topic was Roman history. He loved all things related to Julius Caesar and the Roman Empire. 'Do you know that aqueducts built by the Romans still function today?' He used to say. 'They also invented water proof concrete which was only re-discovered in recent times. Marvellous pieces of engineering and architecture left for posterity and perhaps many more treasures to be discovered'.

Oh my goodness! How can I forget Napoleon Bonaparte? He rattled on and on about all those things with the hope that I developed some curiosity, but I didn't have any interest at all.

I believe he tried to educate me in many ways, because he had a different upbringing to mine. He went to a private school, had a university degree, both his parents also had university degrees, and although they were very polite to me, I must have been a bit of a disappointment to them.

I am the typical uneducated girl who barely finished 10th grade of high school, and went straight to work as an unskilled worker, to have some money and gain independence from my parents. I don't understand why I yearned for independence from my parents; they are good simple people without great ambitions. They provided for the three of us, we never went hungry or needed anything; they didn't pressure any of us to do well academically, because they didn't consider academic instruction to be of great importance, therefore, all of us left school as early as possible. My brother, sister and I felt school was a necessary evil that had to be carried out until year ten, but that was a real struggle, and as long as we were able to read and write that was considered enough.

Our parents never questioned our disinterest in education since they didn't have any, and they didn't appreciate the benefits that a proper education brings to the individual.

I thought everybody lived like us and all I wanted was to get some money to buy lipstick, clothing and girly magazines. I realized people lived and were different to us when I moved to this side of the city, after I found a job at an inner city chocolate factory. I've heard about people who lived north and east of the city to be the wealthy ones, but used to think it was all a myth; from our part of the city we used to call them silver tails, and made fun of their accents, because some of them sounded like they had a hot potato in their mouth when they talked; until then I hadn't seen such wealth.

I also found out that people did behave in a different way, at the beginning I used to call them snobs, until I understood that it's their natural behaviour due to their surroundings, and the different facilities provided to them which make them so different to people from other parts of the city, however, the new knowledge didn't modify my thinking, people like that made me feel uncomfortable, and I disliked their company.

I always managed and still do find the basic individuals who in the same way as me, are like fish out of water trying to adapt to a different existence; some wanted to trade their ordinary ways to be part of a more sophisticated crowd. They dressed better and had modified their accents to be accepted, but always showed in one way or another that they were trying hard to fool others.

All that sophistication and refinement weren't part of my upbringing; it was far removed from my mind that I would ever go out with someone who had those kinds of refinements and privileges in life.

I like to go to the pub and talk football with my pals, I never cooked or had any interest in domestic issues, my life was a big party, my jobs didn't have much responsibility, and the prospects of so called improvements through education were far removed from my psyche. I am a chick with no ambitions that is my problem. All I did then, and to be honest I still do, is buy cheap magazines, cheap shoes, and garments that only last six months.

Perhaps if I had shown some potential about learning the refinements of life, I would've had more chances to gain Franc's parents approval, but it wasn't the case, so eventually their patience won out and certainly, with their encouragement he got rid of me

I refused all Franc efforts to re-educate me. We had very heated arguments which became more frequent as time passed by. We struggled to be together and a distance between us began to emerge. Soon after the dinner fiasco he said: 'I must move out, I've found someone else'.

Although the arguments were rather disturbing, I somehow felt I was going to be with him forever, and hoped that he could become a simpler person, more willing to accommodate my basic mind, instead of being me the one who had to learn and show improvement. That is how we silly women think; we only appreciate what we have when it's gone and too late.

He told me he'd been seeing someone for about six months, and I supposed he wanted to be certain of his feelings before he made the decision to leave me, which after some thought wasn't a difficult choice for him.

I felt like a lightning bolt had hit me and couldn't avoid reacting angrily. I didn't even ask if we could give a second chance to our relationship. I took my handbag and left shutting the door violently as I exited the place. I went to the beach and walked for a while on the promenade, smoked a couple of cigarettes but didn't drop a tear. Then I went to the nearest pub where I knew the publican, and had a couple of drinks.

I thought if I didn't cry it meant that I didn't love him, and I was just accustomed to his presence and kindness. I returned home after a couple of hours a bit more calm, and expected that he was waiting for me, and I could've persuaded him to change his mind, but he'd gone. During those two hours he was able to collect and pack all his belongings, including his beloved books and opera recordings'. The room felt empty without his books; something that I detested and trivialised all of a sudden had value.

Franc left a card on the bed expressing his apologies for the manner in which our liaison had finished, he would have liked to resolve the differences of opinion about life, but he found my thinking impenetrable, almost like a thick bamboo wall, a great obstacle in front of me which stopped me from seeing the brilliancy of a different life path, and all the goodness life has to offer; he didn't think life should be lived in such disharmony.

There is plenty of fish in the ocean I said to myself. Well, that was three years ago and no fish has come to this shore, any fish that arrives here is ridden with emotional problems, or has some sort of mental or physical decay due to the constant consumption of so called recreational drugs, too much alcohol, and some form of paranoia caused by prescription drugs.

I frequent the hip bars and talk to guys, but nobody of good quality shows interest in me, they always seem to prefer younger, better educated girls. I have put on weight and I feel truly unhappy. At times I think that it would've been better to remain where I grew up, now I don't fit anywhere. I am in between two worlds. The ordinary world thinks that I am sophisticated and refined, as they say, 'classy'. The posh world turns the nose up and makes me invisible. I wasn't successful like others who changed their ordinary accents and learnt to utter better sounds avoiding the nasal drawl.

What can I do at this moment? Look at me I am really tragic; I must have gone insane that is why I am talking about my life to a kitten I just bought in a shop.

I hope you stay with me and don't run away. I will feed you and you keep me company. Is that a deal?

I looked at her with my big kitten eyes and purred, that was my way to say thank you for rescuing me. I hope we will be happy together. I'll keep my promise and stay with you.

She didn't know that I was recording the conversation in the same way I would record all my life encounters. It was a recently discovered ability, and I'll make use of it for the rest of my life.

Chapter 2

All the promises and talk about companionship appeared to have fallen through the gaps in the net of life.

My problems began shortly after the girl who rescued me stopped leaving food for me; she didn't come home or simply arrived really late and forgot to bring something for me. There always the dry biscuits she had in her kitchen cabinet compartment, it was then up to someone in the household to put some on a dish for me, luckily most days someone did, but at times people forgot about my existence.

The girl who bought me always smelt of cigarettes, and at other times she had a rancid smell I just couldn't stand; when she smelled like that, I used to run away only returning when she called me for dinner saying: 'puss, puss, come over, come on Franc, I have dinner for you'.

I grew into a young cat and developed friendships with other cats in the neighbourhood. Some felines were truly well looked after by their owners. They were given fresh food every day they were cuddled, and were taken to the vet to have the preventative injection to immunize them against feline influenza, which had killed some of my not so lucky friends. I was very fortunate indeed because I never got sick.

It was the hunger which got me most of the time.

The girl who rescued me was never home, and when she was home she only gave me biscuits, the same ones I was given when I was a kitten while at the shop. To survive I began to chase birds, and at the same time humans began to chase me away from their backyards, it was a desperate situation.

Some of the senior cats told me, that it was very common for humans to lose interest once the kitten begins to grow into an adult.

Well, I can testify that they weren't wrong; from time to time kind individuals invited me to their houses and gave me some of their food. Two human fellows moved to the ground floor flat, they had a restaurant, and once they realized that nobody took care of me, they began to give me some left over morsels, but they weren't interested in me at all, they just did it because they felt sorry for me. After a while I appeared to have exhausted their patience when they became aware that in spite of the food they gave me, I continued to eat the little birds that came to their backyard. They also began to shush me away.

A couple with two children moved to the house next door, an old run down property with a large backyard. They had a dog called Muku, initially the dog wasn't friendly to me, perhaps he thought I was going to eat his food, but when I showed him that I was only interested in the birds that came to his backyard, he was more understanding, and fairly frequently, I could eat a bit of the fresh meat he was given.

His minder used to make a delicious soup with big chunks of meat and vegetables, I liked the overall taste of the concoction, and after he finished his meal, I was allowed to lick the bowl which I enjoyed enormously.

His owner also used to give me some fresh meat, and talked to me in a kind, soft sort of voice.

I visited the grocery shop owner regularly to check whether he had any duties for me to carry out, he always had an opened bag of biscuits; he was generous and gave biscuits to everybody who turned up at his door step, the condition was that if he had detected a rodent in his shop we had to catch it. No need to eat it if we didn't want to, all we had to do was to catch the rodent, and drop it at his feet for him to dispose of it.

The older cats demonstrated an incredible dexterity in catching rodents, so from them I learnt the art of catching them without spilling one drop of blood. It was matter of exerting the correct amount of pressure on the little chap's neck.

It was a good idea to do so, because sometimes the rodents could've eaten poison, and would make the cat that caught it very sick indeed; on some occasions it brought a premature death.

My life wasn't too bad after all, I had freedom to run the length of the street, I had meetings with all the cats who lived around the perimeter, some of them were quite snobbish, especially the ones who had their coat brushed, their teeth cleaned, and had a special bed or slept on their owner's bed.

Out of the blue the girl who bought me said that she had to move out of the house, because she didn't like to live there anymore. She also had met someone and he didn't like cats. What else could she do? She had to leave me behind. There was no choice. It was an opportunity she didn't expect, and perhaps the last chance to find a man. She would come to feed me, not every day of course.

I thought it wouldn't matter or make any difference really, I was wild. I didn't belong to anybody. I'd developed friendships with different shop owners, and with several residents who from time to time threw me a bit of meat or gave me a biscuit.

The girl who bought me left a bowl full of biscuits, maybe she thought the contents left in the bowl would last for a couple of days until she was able to return. As soon as the rodents discovered my food, it was gone in the blink of an eye, and I was left with absolutely nothing. Everybody around me was kind for a while, but as soon as they discovered I didn't have an owner, and I roamed the streets, nobody wanted to know me anymore.

'I was a stray cat, it didn't matter that my coat was of a good colour'.

A thought entered my mind as a way of resolving the stray cat tag; maybe it was worthwhile to pursue the young woman and the two children who lived at the old house next door. Muku the dog liked me, so from that point of view there was no problem.

Perhaps I could adopt them and still stay free, the positive side would be that my meals might have more regularity, and at the same time people wouldn't shush me away.

I decided to begin the adoption process; I started to visit them with more frequency and for longer periods of time, rubbed my scent on her legs and allowed the children to pat me. She gave me food every time I visited, and I began to sit next to the dog when he was sun baking; we had been good mates for a while, basically since Muku arrived in the neighbourhood.

Weeks passed by and her husband noticed my presence, and that she was feeding me more regularly. We can't afford to adopt a stray cat, he said firmly. We like Franc the children said, his wife added that I was such a lovely cat with a beautiful coat. It appeared that everything had been resolved in relation to me.

Chapter 3

The vacant room was rented once more, this time a lovely girl called Marcella arrived.

Her boyfriend, Brett, was a friend of the girl who bought me. Brett suggested to Marcella this place was a better place to live than the one she was living at. Marcella arrived to inspect the room and she liked the view to the beach. Some minutes later I arrived to check her out and to find out what life may bring.

I fell in love with Marcella from the moment I saw her.

She was a real beauty, long dark hair, beautiful smile, she looked like a princess. Her manners were soft, she was very well spoken, and her accent was posh; she appeared very different from the girl who bought me. Marcella was sophisticated, and so deliciously looking, I thought she was the opportunity that would change my life, and I decided to follow my intuition.

Although, I was reasonably friendly, I preferred to know the human before I began to trust.

Marcella moved into the room the girl who bought me had vacated, I liked Marcella's smell, she smelled clean and sweet, she was a happy person, and laughed a lot. She asked who I belonged to because I used to come in and out of the house, and frequently, looked for food. She began to buy food for me, because she said it was terrible to see a cat so neglected. She couldn't understand how a person could be so cruel and uninterested towards a defenseless kitten, barely a year old, with a beautiful coat and so incredibly gentle.

Meanwhile the adoption process I had started with Muku's family next door had to be put on hold temporarily; I had to make a serious assessment about Marcella's potential for adoption, before I made the crucial decision to alter the adoption procedures I had already started.

I continued to visit the children, and responded to their affection with some head butts from time to time, I also kept my friendship with Muku. I sat next to Muku while he enjoyed the morning sun.

Marcella began to feed me daily, so from that point of view my life all of a sudden appeared brighter, and with good prospects for improvement. The girl who bought me arrived at the house sporadically with some tin food, she never brought fresh meat for me like Marcella did, and that was the moment when the arguments with Marcella started, the war of words became very heated.

Marcella was concerned about my wellbeing and the method used to feed me, I was only fed dry biscuits in an irregular pattern with the odd tin food; Marcella didn't mention to the girl who bought me, that she had been feeding me since she moved to the place.

Marcella with strong words continued to tell the girl who bought me that she was cruel and irresponsible. Although the girl who bought me didn't feed me, and didn't look after me either, she didn't want to relinquish her ownership of me. She said, I was the only thing she had. That made Marcella furious, and she used to respond: 'Franc is a living creature, not a thing'. After a while many arguments followed, and through applied pressure Marcella forced the girl who bought me to admit her negligent and irresponsible ways of treating a feline.

Marcella offered a solution that was far removed from my dreams. She was prepared to look after me, as long as the girl who bought me relinquished her ownership, and signed some papers. To my surprise the girl who bought me accepted the deal and from that moment I belonged to Marcella.

My life changed immediately. She continued to bring fresh meat of prime quality for me, so I had a proper dinner every night; for breakfast I had a tin of fish, and I had the odd biscuit before bed.

I began to see her bed as if it was mine as well, and she was happy to share it with me; she used to leave the window open for me to jump in after my night excursions, and during cold nights I cuddled against her for warmth. She brought a special brush with scented cat nip to brush my coat and with affection brushed my coat every day.

Marcella, my princess, used to tell me how beautiful and handsome I was, and it was the first time I experienced a human kiss and a cuddle. She also brought a flea collar with a bell which she tied around my neck; I didn't like it initially, because it had a pungent smell, but eventually, I got used to it. The bell was a warning system for the birds; Marcella thought I was naughty to continue my hunting endeavours since there were no more worries about food or shelter. She told me she loved me and that we will be together forever.

The neighbours who used to chase me away began to observe the changes in me, and all of a sudden I wasn't such a pest; although I continued to eat the odd bird, humans were more tolerant of me.

The lady next door started to say that my behaviour had experienced a change; somehow she thought that I had become haughty since Marcella began to take care of me, and I had stopped loving them. It wasn't the case, I was very grateful for their support and kindness during a difficult time. I still visited them and allowed the children to pat me, but my priorities had changed. I had found my true owner and companion, and I had made up my mind about adopting Marcella.

After Marcella took ownership of me, the girl who had bought me continued her visits to the house frequently, which I found rather disturbing; I used to run away at the sound of her voice, because if she saw me she wanted to pat me, and I disliked her stale smell.

Sometimes she lingered for some hours, especially on the weekend, she liked to talk to whoever was at the house, and we began to hear that her new relationship was on the skids. She recognized another mistake had taken place, and her life once again was in tatters; life with the new bloke only lasted six months after she met him at a bar, and now he had asked her to vacate his premises as soon as possible. They had only known each other for about a week when she moved in with him. This had been the pattern of all her relationships, and had never learnt the lessons life had tried to teach her to improve her existence.

She was miserable and told everybody who listened to her about her current situation; she also wanted to move back to the house, but all the rooms were occupied and at the time nobody had the intention to vacate.

My life had taken the best turn anybody would have ever expected. Marcella told me she had two cats, Lola and Fluffy, they lived with her parents. Lola and Fluffy had been collected from the house of a man who had six cats and couldn't keep them all; with great regret he had to give the kittens away, and her parents after reading a newspaper add decided to call the man. He agreed to a time when her parents and Marcella drove to his house to collect the kittens.

There were three kittens and they would've liked to collect them all, however one kitten went under the washing machine, after a lot of effort it was impossible to make him come out, and

Marcella's parents sadly left with two kittens only.

Marcella said that Lola and Fluffy lived very well and her parents looked after them in an exceptional way; that was the reason she became so irate to find the state of neglect I was in.

Her parent's house was roomy, Lola and Fluffy had a cat door with a marble threshold, and they were free to go in and out of the house at their will.

She said she loved them because they had arrived when she was eight years old, and since she was an only child she felt they were like her brother and sister. Her parents lived in an up market area also close to the sea; she often talked about the magnificent view, and how quiet the street was since it was a cul-de-sac; that was the reason Lola and Fluffy had so much freedom, cars weren't a problem to their safety.

On the other hand with the help of the older felines I had become very street wise, I learnt not to cross the road without having a good look first, to see if any car came my way, but in general I didn't have to cross streets. Most humans appeared to know all the felines who lived in the neighbourhood and they were happy with our presence, except when we ate the little birds.

Everything was at my paw tips, the butcher, the general store and most of the friends who hung around with me seemed to live on the same side of the street.

Marcella's parents came to see the place she had moved into, and to meet me as well, because Marcella had talked a lot about her new found feline. I was introduced to them and as usual I was distant and aloof; they patted me with affection and said some kind words.

Life couldn't be better. I loved Marcella and I knew she loved me. We looked after each other. As soon as I heard the sound of her voice I ran to see her, it was the best moment of my day. I knew the time she returned from work and I was eagerly waiting for her every afternoon. She always came home and fed me before she went out with her friends or with Brett.

From the moment Marcella and I adopted each other, she was very particular about my health, and we made regular visits to the vet for vaccination, to give me worm tablets, to check my teeth, or any small scar created by some altercation with other cat. It was the first time I experienced all this love and attention.

A good friend of Marcella picked us up one day in his red Porsche, I had to be taken to the vet for a check-up and a vaccine, when we arrived at the premises everybody looked at me and they said: 'this is the cat that travels in a Porsche'. Isn't he handsome!

I wasn't sure whether they referred to me or to the man and his Porsche because he was a well known personality, fairly charismatic and good looking.

Marcella's neighbours also began to talk about the immense changes this girl brought into my life, I felt incredibly privileged and proud every time I heard something said. People used to say: that cat was a stray, but he somehow managed to find someone to look after him. At the same time my coat became silky and soft with a good shine, and I felt amazingly happy.

I told every feline who was my friend that I had an owner, and that she loved me and cared for me, in the same truly exceptional way they were looked after by their owners. They always looked at me with certain disbelief.

Those pussycats meowed and closed their eyes like saying 'how did you manage that'.

The man and his red Porsche were the means of transport for me, every time we had to go somewhere he was ready to take us there; he liked Marcella a lot, but respected the fact that she was going out with Brett who was a friend of his. What a pity I thought, it would have made her parents really happy if Marcella had decided to go out with him instead of Brett.

He was a much better person, not because of his red Porsche, but he had a good background and he was truly a nice man; he treated Marcella with kindness and respect and he liked me too. I also liked the excursions in his Porsche on Saturday or Sunday afternoon when he used to visit Marcella, and offered to take us for a drive, I stood up on Marcella's lap and looked out of the window, when the car stopped at the intersections people used to look at us and they said: 'look at that cat in that Porsche, isn't he handsome!' I was never sure if I was the handsome one, or the Porsche, or the man driving it.

I said it was a pity that Marcella didn't select the man and his Porsche as her boyfriend instead of Brett. Marcella met

Brett at a party long before a friendship developed; she still lived at her parent's house when Brett began to pursue her. One morning there was a knock on the door and a voice called to Marcella, her mother went to the door and found Brett holding the milk bottles which had been delivered that morning. He asked for Marcella, he introduced himself and was invited in.

He sat down and ordered Marcella to fetch him a glass of water, while Marcella brought the glass of water, he told her parents about his trips to Cuba and his affinity with Fidel Castro's regime. He spoke a bit of Spanish and was very taken by the communist idea. That was the only time her parents had the opportunity to talk to him, and curiously enough they warned Marcella about him.

They thought he would be a person difficult to get rid of once she started going out with him, but as usual she didn't listen because it was only their intuition.

Marcella in general had the idea that whoever she went out with was to be kept away from her parent's scrutiny, because they were difficult to please, she didn't want to see they only wanted the best for her.

Her parents expected her to go out with a person who had a reasonably good level of education, and good manners; but unfortunately, that expectation appeared not to be a priority for Marcella, she usually, seemed to gravitate to certain type of individuals who were quite unsuitable; her parents couldn't understand what attracted her interest to a guy like Brett.

The relationship Marcella had with Brett, the chap who had brought her to this dusty place began to crumble. I couldn't believe why this guy didn't pay enough attention to this lovely girl. They seemed to get along well, they went away and had fun, but he was a sort of strange person.

Brett was a successful photographer. He had achieved his fifteen minutes of fame, as the photographer who was able to photograph a famous footballer while he had a shower after a football game; the photo appeared in a tabloid newspaper with the result that Brett was sued as well as the newspaper he worked for. The incident was splashed on newspapers, and television.

Brett's personal life was a bit of mess, some childhood problems affected his life and often he was quite despondent. I knew for sure that Marcella's parents didn't think he was a good choice for her; such a beautiful girl who had the best education money could buy, had love and affection as well, deserved in their eyes someone more refined and educated.

Marcella's mother indeed tried to understand Brett's odd manner, and joined them for lunch as a way of getting to know a bit more about him, but at the end she gave up. Marcella's father said it was a waste of time and didn't give him a chance.

There were other changes that coincidentally arrived at the same time. Another girl moved to the premises, Marcella had invited her to move into the building because she didn't want the girl who had bought me to move in when a room was vacated. Marcella couldn't tolerate her. Unfortunately, the new girl was hostile towards me from the very beginning, and although, she knew of my existence prior to her moving into the premises, she began to complain and bother Marcella about me leaving fur everywhere, and that she was allergic to cats.

Marcella had heated arguments with this girl. It appeared to be that the source of the argument was my presence in the house, and the girl's intention was to get rid of me at all cost, however, Marcella's love for me prevailed.

The relationship with Brett deteriorated further and her place of work was unsatisfactory; although she was well paid, she was critical of the designer and argued with him nonstop about his designs, when in reality it wasn't up to her to discuss those issues, since he didn't ask for her opinion, and she wasn't even an assistant designer.

Against her parent's advice Marcella accepted a job in a town approximately three hours from the capital. That job had all the hallmarks of a disaster. Marcella would be isolated from her so called friends, her parents also would be away from her, and although, the job appeared interesting it brought her less money. All in all, it wasn't a wise decision to make.

Marcella, a budding designer with great talent and ability was throwing many opportunities away. No amount of persuasive words from her parents made her change her mind.

The main reason for her to make this silly decision was to get away from Brett who had become in a way, a nightmare.

Had she mentioned it to her parents they would have found a better solution. Marcella thought she could find her own way to resolve the problem, and in her mind the best way was to move to a distant place, so Brett wouldn't bother her anymore.

By this time her parents had sold their house in the upscale suburb, and had bought land close to a national park, it was a large block of land with a magnificent native garden and the house had to be built.

Meanwhile, her parents had to move to temporary premises close to the new property. The construction was underway, and the new house was completed in record time. By then Marcella had left her job, and decided to move for a short period of time to her parent's new house before moving to the town where her new job was going to be, the problem was that I didn't fit in the picture because of Fluffy and Lola.

Their advanced age was a bit of a concern, they were already nineteen years old and it was my understanding they were extremely pampered.

Marcella's parents thought that it would be unfair on them to bring a young springy pussycat into the house; obviously, they didn't have a good knowledge of my gentle personality and my great adaptability to any circumstance.

While Marcella found a place to live I was left in a cat hotel; expensive and very nice. I spent a month there; I developed friendships with other cats whose owners had gone on holidays. The owners of the cat hotel were kind and the premises were absolutely impeccable. We had cushions and a little house of our own, we could sit on a perch to watch the outdoors; during the night there were heaters to take the chill out of the air, the food was good and varied. It wasn't a bad time at all, although I missed Marcella.

A month passed by and Marcella found a place to live. What a dump it was, I was accustomed to live in dusty, smelly, run down places, but this one was the pits.

I was picked up at the cat hotel, and with Marcella's belongings her parents drove three hours to the place she had rented. We all checked the premises, and neither her parents nor I could believe that a girl who was accustomed to live in absolute comfort could ever contemplate to live in such a place.

There is no public transport from here, her parents said. How are you going to commute to work? Let's have a look how long it takes to get there by car, and with feline in tow, we all drove to her future work place. It took 30 minutes.

Marcella, as we said before you need a car, how are you going to live in this isolation? Let's hope for the best, we are sure you have it all sorted out. After helping Marcella to unload everything and put each item where she wanted them to be, they left, it was late in the afternoon and they had three hours drive to return home.

We had been living in this dump for nearly two weeks and it was truly awful. The smell was more rancid than anywhere else I've ever been; a strong acrid smell everywhere gave me nausea and I yearned to be let out in the fresh air. I had to wait until Marcella returned home in the afternoon to go out.

I had Marcella and she for sure could count on me, but the horrible place was driving me insane, to the point that after countless efforts I managed to escape. Marcella arrived from work one afternoon and she was in a fit of panic when she couldn't find me.

I had escaped and was under the house waiting for her, but I fell asleep and didn't hear her calls; she looked under the house and said: 'what are you doing there? You had me sick with worry I thought a snake had eaten you'. When she said snake I jumped out of my skin and ran towards Marcella who hugged me with great love and gave me dinner.

We lived there for several months until it began to rain, and water started to penetrate through the ceiling, Marcella talked to her mother about the problem, and I think the advice was to take the opportunity to terminate the contract, which she did.

We moved to a place by the sea, it was a new house near a national park. The little house was freshly painted, there was plenty of light, the smell was fresh and salty; unfortunately, I couldn't go out because I was considered to be a menace to the many birds that visited the garden.

Brett's torment continued and at times it appeared that Marcella was the victim of a stalker. He phoned her regularly, sent her parcels, and harassed her nonstop. He did interfere in her life, and was beginning to make her feel nervous; she thought he could've appeared at her door at any minute and that made her panic.

He happened to be an individual difficult to get rid of as her parents had warned her after they met him.

Marcella also had the belief that her so call friends from school days would visit her on weekends, but the reality was that nobody cared about her, and soon she realized that real friends are rare; her parents had tried to make her understand that her chosen friends treated her with disrespect since school days, the sad reality was that at the end they had been correct in their assumptions.

Her parents many times had said to Marcella to be more discerning and careful when choosing friends; she wanted to be popular at all cost, and was easily misled with the idea that everybody was sincere, which wasn't the case.

Marcella's mother often said to her: 'Marcella, there are lovely people out there, why do you always gravitate towards those types of individuals who are just fakes? Can you see those girls you call friends from your school days, don't give a hoot about you. They make fun of you, and they treat you with disrespect. What is stopping you from seeing the reality of it all?'

Marcella's many trips to the city to see her friends didn't bring happiness to my life either, and I was often very lonely during the weekends when she decided to leave.

A neighbour fed me with the meat Marcella had left prepared, and gave me breakfast, it wasn't the same. I waited anxiously by the door, I knew the sound of every car that passed by, the hours didn't pass fast enough to bring Marcella home.

Marcella fortunately, found out who was giving information about her to Brett, and finally she severed the connection with that person; her telephone number was changed and at work she asked the girl who answered the phone to say she didn't work there anymore when Brett called. It took a while to get rid of him, after a long time it appeared that she had succeeded and he was out of her life for good.

We had moved into a clean, new two bedroom town house, freshly painted and full of light, but it was a strange place. Marcella couldn't sleep well, she used to wake up with the feeling someone was walking along the corridor in between the bedrooms and the living room; on many occasions we even heard footsteps.

I was often spooked by a strong presence; my tail's fur stood up and Marcella observed me while I directed my eyes towards the corner of the room where I felt the presence. I also howled and quickly ran away from the room. It was the same corner where she felt the presence as well. She asked me: Franc what is it?

Marcella felt very nervous, and began to buy some smelly sticks from the crystal shop; the sales woman at the shop told her that the sweet smell of sandalwood would give her some tranquillity, and it would make the spirits move away.

Marcella's mother came to visit and stayed with us, unable to sleep on the sofa because she felt really spooked, moved to Marcella's bed and the three of us slept for a few hours until the strange sensation that someone was walking into the room happened once more. I jumped off the bed briskly and Marcella and her mother were disturbed.

Marcella was quite settled in her job, she liked what she was doing, and although the people she worked for were rather difficult, she managed to develop a good business relationship, she also made friends with a young married couple who resided in a nearby town, and they were very good to her; she worked at the same place with Marcella, the husband taught surfing to tourists during his free time. After Marcella met them she was more relaxed; I guess she didn't feel so lonely because at least she had someone to talk to, and the long absences from me didn't happen with the same frequency.

CHAPTER 4

One day Marcella said: 'Franc, would you like to have a sister?'

Someone at work found a little kitten, she'd been dumped in the bush, is lovely and apparently house trained. He can't keep her, because he has four pussycats already, and can't afford the cost involved with one more.

I looked at her with my big round eyes and purred.

The very next day I had a sister whose health wasn't very good. While she had been dumped in the bush, she had to fend for herself, and was malnourished; a tick was found on her neck, and she had a heart murmur, so she had to go to the veterinary hospital for treatment.

She was away for a week until the vet made her feel better, Marcella called the surgery every afternoon after she returned home until the day she was told that the kitten could be collected the next day. Marcella picked her up and that afternoon when they arrived home, I realized that my new sister had lots of energy to play and she was talkative, inquisitive, curious, and asked many questions.

Marcella called her Mia and she responded fairly quickly to her new name, we didn't know what she was called before we adopted her. Very pretty feline, black long coat with a white belly and white paws, she had white markings around the neck, similar to a Tasmanian devil I had seen on a television documentary.

Her face also had marks, in between her eyes there was a white mark that looked like a flame, and around her eyes there were black lines like the ones Queen Cleopatra had around hers. I had learnt about Queen Cleopatra, because I had seen her pictures on Marcella's books.

Mia's nose was pink, she had gorgeous green eyes, and when she walked her tail pointed up and was curly at the tip. My life was certainly complete, I wasn't lonely anymore, Marcella looked after us, and we were company for her as well.

My new sister drove me crazy sometimes, she jumped and ran everywhere, she talked all the time, and unlike me, she didn't have the need to sleep as many hours as I did. I felt exhausted.

I developed great affection for her; she was very cute and was growing healthier by the minute with the good food and care Marcella provided for her. She had to go to the vet several times for checkups; the heart murmur apparently, was quite serious and had to be kept under control.

I assured her that we were in good hands and this human was kind and loving, Mia had a bit of paranoia, and didn't like to be cuddled, and kissed, in a way she was very much like I was, before Marcella began to take care of me.

The big difference was that Mia had been hurt profoundly; her physical problems had been resolved, but she also had the psychological scars which perhaps would take a long time to heal. No matter how much love Marcella gave her, she was distrustful and aloof.

Marcella and I thought she had been tormented. We felt very sorry for her, such a pretty and sweet pussycat. Why anybody would torment a little kitten and then damp her in the bush?

Eighteen months had passed since Marcella and I had arrived in this town; she decided that it was time to return to the city, so she began to search for a new job. The couple she had befriended moved back to the city, and that inspired her to make a change. It was difficult to arrange interviews because she had to find an excuse to remain in the city until Monday.

She finally found a job which from the beginning looked quite unsuitable, but decided to take it as an interim solution to get out of that town.

Marcella saw her parents and told them about the decision to return to the city, and she would've liked for the three of us to move into their roomy house, but unfortunately, after Lola's death the year before, Fluff's health had deteriorated to the point that he was quite frail. Her parents thought that it wouldn't be fair to Fluffy to introduce two young felines.

Fluffy was much pampered and at the age of twenty one, he would've been unhappy with our presence. Once more

Marcella left us at a cat hotel which wasn't really a luxurious hotel as the one she'd chosen previously; it was at the vet's premises.

We were fed and our coats were brushed by the trainee nurses, sometimes we couldn't go outside our cages at all; other times the nurses took us out for a couple of minutes during the day if they weren't too busy attending to other patients. It wasn't a happy experience, I became ill and after I was accustomed to fresh meat for dinner every day, I was put on a diet of dry biscuits which I ate, because there was no other choice. Marcella did contact the vet to check on our wellbeing, but that wasn't enough for us; it was so terribly depressing.

Marcella lived with her parents until she found a place of her own, close to the work she had accepted. After three long months, Marcella appeared one day with her mother to collect us. We were incredibly happy to see her, and we began the drive to our new home.

We arrived at a fairly small place, dark and squashy, no trees or garden to look at, and not a lot of sunshine to enjoy either. Marcella's mother hadn't seen the place and was astonished that she would pay to live in such horrid environment.

She said it was totally unsuitable for us as well as for her; a horrendous location, near striptease joints, seedy bars and not a ray of sun for us. We were happy to be with Marcella; however, life wasn't going to be smooth.

Marcella's job was a disaster and from the very beginning it was difficult for her to accept the new circumstances. To begin with, the first payment she received was greatly reduced from the amount of remuneration she had agreed to, and her complaints were ignored. Instead of looking for a better job she took all the bad things the owners or managers dished out to her. Extended work hours, weekend work and a dreadful environment.

To make matters worse she was moved from the area where all the office personnel were located to another floor. To her surprise she was transferred to where the storemen and packers were located. She tried to make the best out of it, but her life wasn't good at that time.

Her parents were appalled at her lack of enthusiasm to get on her feet, and to find a job more suitable to her abilities. It appeared to be that Marcella had lost her confidence and energy.

She had no boyfriend, the so called friends, the ones she knew for a long time deserted her completely; work was a disaster and the place she lived in was like a prison cell. We did our part to cheer her up, and she never failed us with affection and good food. From time to time her mother had to come to the rescue; there were inspections every quarter and the three of us had to exit the place, and any trace of feline habitation had to be erased, otherwise, she would have had to pay a fine or vacate the premises.

It was stressful, because the three of us with Marcella's mother had to sit in the car for about two hours while the inspection was carried out.

The difficult part was to get us out of the building without being noticed; at the end of the two hours the mood was different and we felt very comfortable in that smart little car, so comfortable, we didn't want to return to the flat, because during those two hours we went to a park where there were birds and trees and we saw the sun light.

Her mother always gave her encouragement to change jobs, and to look for a better place for all of us, but she lacked the energy to better her life and ours.

Marcella used to come home and while she prepared our food, she talked about the problems she had that day, we listened and at the end we purred and gave her head butts.

Life wasn't good for anybody.

After she carried out her duties with us, she used to call her mum to tell her about the horrors she had endured during the day.

Marcella met a new chap, a lawyer who had a job with a judge. This fellow travelled away from the city on a regular basis. He was truly interested in Marcella, while in the city, he invited Marcella to dinners, and parties, and she seemed to enjoy his company, but something wasn't quite right. He had seen Marcella's place, and curiously enough made the same comment her mother made about it.

It was nearly a year since we had moved to that flat, and Marcella decided to listen to her mother's advice to find a better place for all of us. Her mother said one day while she visited: 'Marcella this awful place will only bring you more misfortune, until you find a place with better energies, nothing in your life will progress'. Think about it, since you moved here you've had problems at work, with friends, you have been constantly unwell, and face it, this isn't the most glamorous place to live, it is like a box, dark, dingy, surrounded by striptease joints, seedy bars and we haven't mentioned how unfair it is to keep Franc and Mia in this horrible environment.

Marcella finally found a new place, a flat not far away from where we lived, according to her mother it was another place in the same down market suburb which was full of striptease joints, bars and just around the corner from a methadone clinic.

'What is you infatuation with this part of town?' She used to ask her.

Marcella made an appointment to see the flat and asked her mother to join her; the day of the appointment Fluffy died around 11am. Marcella's mother called to tell her about the sad news and declined to make the appointment which was scheduled for the afternoon. Marcella was upset that her mum couldn't make it, but for us the sad news of Fluffy passing was our salvation, within a couple of weeks we moved to Marcella's parent's spacious and beautiful home.

CHAPTER 5

The scent of Fluffy, the feline was there, and so was his presence. We also felt the sadness and the grief Marcella's parents were experiencing.

We tried to be quiet and kept out of their way, not because they didn't treat us with kindness, but because we sensed their grief, they were mourning their beloved pussycat. After all Fluffy had lived with them since he was six weeks old, that was twenty two years from the time he and Lola had been picked up at the man's house.

We all had adjustments to make and a brand new life began for us; it was such a lovely environment with birds of all sorts passing by, some large ones quite noisy, as well as the little ones with blue feathers that hovered in the bush undergrowth. There were many native animals who roamed in the garden day and night; I couldn't believe my eyes, it was almost like a dream after the dull life we experienced in that barren environment, we had lived for a long year.

Mia was in a panic, the sounds from the bush made her very nervous, and she remained in Marcella's bedroom all day and night, she didn't venture outside for many days. She was truly scared until I managed to convince her to come to the guest room at night.

We went downstairs to the guest bedroom to observe the wild life. Possums with their big brush tails stopped in front of us on the other side of the very large windows, and we growled and hissed at each other.

Mia initially stood next to me frozen with panic, but I assured her there wasn't anything to worry and it was fun; when the bandicoots saw us on the other side of the window they jumped nervously and ran away; big bush rats also moved nervously, wallabies didn't take any notice of us unless they were young and inexperienced.

We also went downstairs during the day; the odd rabbit came from the property next door which was infested with them, in a way the infestation provided food for the goanna, but the rabbits didn't venture past the open bush areas. When the weather was warm large goannas walked slowly by the side of the house, we also saw an echidna with her little inward twisted feet she waddled past the window while she smelt the ground, and didn't even notice us.

It was a constant parade of diverse animals. There were several young bush turkeys who didn't pay any attention to us, they just passed in front of the window without a care in the world, there was a lyre bird who jumped on the terrace to inspect the planter boxes, after she messed up the soil she moved close to the kitchen door, deposited a dropping on the tiles and moved away; I'd seen the lyre bird, and decided that the following time I would be ready to stare and hiss at her in the same manner we used to stare at the possums.

One morning after the morning coffee break, I saw the lyre bird through the glass door, and ran towards her, by the time I approached the door I was the terrified one. As soon as she detected my presence she lifted her legs and hit the glass like thunder; my heart almost jumped out of its cavity. That was one of my scary moments, so I didn't bother with that bird anymore.

Although the house was full of light and the sun penetrated well into the open spaces, initially, I went downstairs to hide in the most distant corner of the guest bedroom walk-in wardrobe. I was totally out of view. On many occasions Marcella's mother called me, but of course I didn't answer, when I was found she always told me there was no need to hide. She reminded me that it was lovely and sunny upstairs, lifted me up from the shelf and moved me upstairs in front of a window where she had arranged a bean bag.

The problem was that we could smell Fluffy the feline, but we couldn't see him, it took a while to understand that although his spirit was in the house his physical presence was gone. It took some time to sort out the feline etiquette to follow at such times, and while we found a solution, we really didn't know what to do with our new surroundings. Once I felt comfortable with our new situation and discovered it was wonderful to sit by the window, I just took to it with great gusto.

To sun bake by the many windows facing the large pool, and to be able to look at the lizards that lived under the window frame, was a great source of entertainment. I used to run from window to window as the lizards darted outside on the terrace tiles, the warm terracotta tiles were perfect for the lizards to warm up while the sun was out, and I watched them with delight.

The stairway window was an amazing platform to watch the birds, a tree with blue berries was a great attraction to many large birds like the currawongs; those black, big birds with yellow eyes, glossy feathers and a ferocious beak, used to stop there and didn't take any notice of me, they ignored my presence completely as they continued to eat the berries.

Noir and Pierre, the magpie couple, who had lived here since Marcella's parents bought the property, also used the tree when they arrived in the afternoon for a feed of little pieces of meat and some sunflower seeds. A couple of cockatoos which didn't have a name arrived each morning for a breakfast of sunflower seeds; very friendly, and Marcella's mother could touch the crest and wings of one of them.

The rainbow lorikeets also arrived in the morning; very noisy and from a feline point of view a delicious morsel, but I wasn't given the chance to get near them. I could only observe them from the distance, and I was told not to torment them because they could break their wings. The beautiful king parrots, dressed in their red, green, and blue plumage, also began to make their presence felt, everybody appeared to like the sun flower seeds.

Marcella's mother talked to the birds, patted their back and tickled their neck. They all continued to eat the seeds without flapping an eyelash.

I used to get delirious over those birds. I could remember the taste of their little bodies; although, I was well fed I was still wild at heart. Slowly, slowly my bad habits would go deep into my subconscious, and sometime later I could watch them and remain calm, but my jaws still clicked out of control.

The brown doves were my greatest temptation as well as the lorikeets; they were fed on the balcony floor, they were so close yet too far. The glass was the barrier that protected them from my attempts to catch them.

We had bad habits because Marcella never objected to us scratching the furniture, her furniture was old, maybe that was the reason; however, Marcella's parents furnishings were exclusive and of high quality, since we couldn't understand the difference between one or the other, we scratched everything to their annoyance; expensive leather sofas were left with deep claw marks and rips on the leather, fine Persian rugs began to show threads protruding from their otherwise soft texture.

We were in real trouble and had to learn fast, we also had to put into practice all the new rules. It wasn't easy for me, a wild feline with bad habits. I sensed that Marcella's parents liked us and wanted the best for us, we also felt welcome from the moment we arrived, but took a while to adjust to the new life.

Marcella's mother bought a scratching post made of carpet, and Mia liked it immediately, however I didn't like it, so she had to find an alternative more suited to my needs; she brought some smart looking squares of dark grey carpet, and placed them in strategic places, she then took me to them and showed me that it was fine to scratch them with my claws, she called my claws toe nails.

Time passed by and we all got used to each other, Marcella's mother fed us in the afternoon and her father fed us in the morning; we began to settle into a nice routine, that was when Marcella began to go out more often.

We spent most of the time with her parents who slowly began to be our parents as well. Both of them had their offices at home, and we began to visit each office to help with their work.

Marcella's father had a lot of files in boxes, so Mia decided to sleep on the files, and I slept on the side of a filing cabinet which received a good deal of morning sun; after lunch when the sun began to move west, I moved to the other office, but Mia remained in the boxes, she looked like a paper weight holding the files.

They both came and went as their routines demanded but we were always well looked after. Sometimes, when both of them went out on business we waited on the ground floor by the internal garage door, as they arrived we both received a pat, and food followed depending on the time of the day, otherwise a little morsel was given to us.

Life was truly magic. In the morning during coffee break we began to go out on the terrace, Mia was well behaved, her bush experience when she was dumped as a kitten wasn't a good one; she had suffered hunger, loneliness, fear, as well as illness, and those experiences contributed to her good behaviour, but I was a bit of a problem, because I always wanted to run after the wildlife. My wild instincts hadn't disappeared yet.

Time and time again I was warned not to do it, but my obstinate ways were difficult to overcome; it was explained to me that I could get hurt, maybe a goanna or a snake would eat me, but I didn't believe them. Maybe it was a way to frighten me, and therefore stop me from being wild.

The other problem was the ticks, which are common in that part of the city, because of the natural bush which remains in pristine condition since the first Europeans arrived. Apparently, there are plants and animals which rarely exist anywhere else in the city's periphery. I didn't believe any of that. A strong feline scared of ticks, snakes, and goannas, it wasn't me.

I had to experience all that and the day would certainly arrive when I could jump into the bush and check it all out. I could face anything in front of me no matter the size.

I had forgotten ticks make us very sick and sometimes were the cause of premature death and at other times paralysis; Mia had the experience of a tick attached to her neck under her thick coat, it happened when she was a kitten dumped in the bush, when she returned home from hospital, all the fur around her neck was shaven and she looked like a poodle; it was then when she faced the prospect of death, the prompt attention from an experienced vet saved her life.

It was a serene household, so it was strange when arguments surfaced sporadically between Marcella and her parents. She owned a little car which she'd purchased while we lived in the small town, unfortunately, she hadn't paid the vehicle registration fees, and in spite of her parent's warnings about the problems she could face with the law, didn't listen. Instead, as always, she became annoyed at them for trying to make her accept responsibilities; she responded with a dreadful and dismissive manner.

A couple of months passed by until one day on her way to work a traffic policeman stopped her. She was driving on the lane designated for public transport, such as buses and taxis, in an unregistered car. The policeman removed the number plates from the car, and gave her a hefty traffic infringement fine; she was lucky the police didn't cancel her license as well. The problems had arrived as she had been warned.

The worse aspect could have been avoided if she had listened. Marcella was angry about what happened, and after the policeman made her drive the car to the nearest street, she called her mother to tell her about the incident.

She was furious at the police and the world for the incident. Ordered her mother to organize a tow truck because she didn't want to leave the car without number plates on the street; she had to pick her up and then take her to work, which was literarily half way across the city. During pick hour traffic it would've taken her mother close to an hour to drive from home to where Marcella was, and to drive from where Marcella found herself without a car to her work place, it would've taken another hour or more at that time of the day, and that didn't include the time required to return home.

Her mother refused to do what Marcella, in an angry and bad manner had demanded of her; also reminded her of the many times the subject of the unpaid registration was mentioned, and her aggressive response towards them every time it was suggested that it was wrong not to pay the vehicle registration, because the insurance wouldn't cover the cost of an accident.

It was a costly exercise for Marcella who had to organize a tow truck to collect the car, bring it to her parent's house, and place it in the driveway until the traffic infringement fees were paid. She hadn't told her parents that she had an enormous telephone bill that reached thousands of dollars, and compounded with the traffic infringement, it would take her a long time to be able to pay those bills.

Marcella's parents usually said to her: 'if you only had a good manner when you create a problem, we would go out of our way to help you, but with that ferocious aggression and expectation that we have to resolve your problems, you make your life more complicated'.

The following day marked the beginning of a daily routine when one of her parents had to drive her to the bus stop, where she could catch the bus to go to work in the morning, and also pick her up in the afternoon. The trip to reach her work took two hours each way. She was sitting in a bus for four or more hours every day. She was crazy not to listen, sort of like me; ignored advice which was offered with love and best intentions at heart.

Marcella's lawyer friend gave her the flick. In passing she mentioned that he expected too much attention from her, and that he was tiring as well as too square. She also made the comment that she couldn't argue with him. Her parents were perplexed.

'Why would you want to argue? He appeared to like you', was her parent's response.

We thought he was disappointed by her lack of responsibility, and perhaps she started to argue when he expressed his opinion in relation to the traffic incident, and she didn't agree with him.

Marcella continued to work long hours and also found a second job with a silver service company; it would help her to earn extra income needed to pay the debts incurred with the car fiasco as well as the exorbitant telephone bill.

Her parents didn't help her financially this time as they had done in the past, because until this moment, she hadn't demonstrated any intention to behave in a sensible manner, or to be responsible for her actions; the only visible change was the level of aggression which seemed to increase every time a crisis appeared.

Once more she brought another problem on herself by her own stubborn and irresponsible behaviour. This time her parents told her that for a person in her thirties, this was the opportunity to learn that every action brings a consequence, maybe she didn't agree with them.

It was as if Marcella went out of her way to complicate her life, and things didn't improve for her either, she disliked her job, had arguments with the person she had to report to, and every afternoon we had to listen to all her complaints; when her mother suggested that the cause of her problems perhaps was her own doing, and that she ought to be more attentive to her reactions, she became aggressive and began to shout.

I hadn't seen that side of Marcella's character, because we had lived on our own for three years, therefore, there was no way of knowing about those idiosyncrasies. This ugly trait didn't affect the love I had for her, I still ran to the sound of her voice and so did my sister Mia. The problems continued to increase for her at work until she was asked to leave; she found another job almost immediately.

Marcella was always in a bad mood, and showed a lot of aggression and hostility towards her parents. It seemed to us that she blamed them for all the negative aspects that had appeared around her.

She never lifted a finger to do anything at home, by this time her mother was buying the meat for us, and all the responsibility had fallen on Marcella's parents. We thought it wasn't fair, but Mia and I were truly happy with our new life. We had found a secure, beautiful place to live, we felt loved, and we had fun with the variety of distractions available to us. Slowly we began to be more detached from Marcella.

She was rebuilding her finances and paying for her fines which were quite substantial; meanwhile the little car was parked in the driveway, and the weeds began to invade the interior.

Her parents suggested the car to be sold as soon as the traffic incident occurred, but she refused. She arrived at a point where she was working to pay the car finance, her traffic penalties, and the phone bill; her temper wasn't the best, and heated arguments with her parents were more common than not. We just listened, ran away and hid in a corner.

Marcella met many people while she worked at those silver service jobs, being such a pretty girl with a good personality she attracted a lot of attention. Among those people, she met a man who began to contact her and invited her out. He had a shop somewhere in the business district, his shop sold women's fashion. She was highly impressed by him and his stories, as well as the people he knew because of his business.

He began to ask Marcella to design fashion items for him from the moment they met and she obliged.

On one occasion she spent about four hours designing garments for him after she had worked all day. She finished the designs at around 10pm and the man thanked her; then said that he couldn't bring her home because he had to meet some friends. Marcella took a taxi, and by the time she arrived home, she was fuming. Marcella arrived home close to midnight, and was so angry about the episode, that the next day decided to tell her mother about the incident and asked for her opinion.

She replied that the creature wasn't worth a minute of her time, and not to see him again, because he appeared to be a user. A decent person doesn't conduct business in this manner, and is not the base to start a relationship either.

Marcella continued to see him to her parent's surprise, and began to spend more time with him. She didn't return home on weekends and sometimes during the week she also stayed away. We didn't mind it, because Mia and I had decided to sleep with our new parents, they had a great big bed and we could stretch across while they struggled to fit their legs.

Many times they had to visit Jodie the osteopath, for their bones and muscles to be relieved from aches and pains caused by falling asleep with their bodies all twisted, while we stretched comfortably. We had already felt their love for us, and how much they cared about our wellbeing.

Marcella was already thirty three years old, if she didn't want to listen to wise advice, nothing could be done about it, and all of us accepted her decision. One day Marcella said she would like to introduce the man, which she did. After he left she asked her mother about her opinion.

Her mother said: 'do you really want my opinion? You may not like what I have to say'.

'Yes tell me. Please'

Well, her mother said: 'he looks like death warmed up. Is he really fifty six years old? He looks ancient, unhealthy, and doesn't have a pleasant manner. You are such a pretty girl and many good guys would love to go out with you. Why are you so determined to spoil your life? He is too old for you, a name dropper, and there is more to him, maybe he is a person with a lot of baggage'.

Marcella agreed with her mother's comments, and didn't seem affected by them, but she continued to see the man and it appeared to us that she had made a decision.

We didn't know a lot of things about Marcella, for us she was our rescuer, and we were always very grateful for her efforts to keep us together, which at times was quite difficult due to the financial situation.

The car, after two years in the driveway, was finally sold and Marcella was a bit free of financial problems; of course she had more disposable income and began to buy excessive amounts of clothing and shoes; her room was in a mess with many items thrown on the floor, and this was a constant source of arguments with her mother.

Her parents decided to turn a blind eye to her spending; it had been hard on Marcella for about two years while she paid her debts. She had worked very hard, and it was a great credit to her at a time when many people her age having accumulated big debts opted for the easy way out, and declared to be bankrupt.

A source of disagreement was that she didn't help on anything related to the house, the cleaning woman left and everything fell on her mother's shoulders; Marcella was quite uninterested in her parents work, and refused to help with the small tasks assigned to her.

They felt she had to contribute to something, but Marcella refused to listen and continued to waste a lot of money on going out, clothing, shoes, and magazines.

Her mother grew tired of her behaviour as well as the wasteful ways, consequently, decided to ask Marcella to give her one hundred dollars per week, and told her that if the money wasn't spent on paying the new cleaner, the dollars would be there for her to use in case she wanted to go on a holiday. It appeared that Marcella only heard that the money would be there if she wanted to go on a holiday, she didn't want to hear that the money could be spent to pay the cleaner. She had only given her mother cash for ten weeks; the money was kept in an envelope. This incident would be the source of a horrendous argument.

Marcella's parents decided to go on a short holiday, they needed a break from the hard work both of them put into their business, as well as the stress Marcella was imposing on them on a regular basis. Her constant altercations about insignificant matters created a difficult environment to live.

I wasn't aware of previous problems when they had gone on holidays, and I wasn't aware either that Marcella always created a scene before they left or on their return. Apparently, this was an issue that in spite of Marcella's age had continued since her childhood. We were about to witness a very ugly scene soon after their return.

Marcella wanted the man she had been seeing for some months to keep her company while her parents were absent, this was a fair request, and also would give Mia and me the opportunity to meet him; we had heard a lot about him.

Her parents agreed, they trusted that if he stayed with Marcella, his company perhaps would remove the usual source of an argument, whatever the cause was; it didn't occur to them that the cause was deeply embedded in her psyche.

There was no argument before their departure, it was a good sign; perhaps Marcella had finally begun to modify her behaviour. Marcella said that she would meet Peter at the shop instead of leaving straight from work as she normally did. That meant that they would return home after 7pm.

Her mother was concerned about us and the long, lonely day we might have, also she felt sorry that we wouldn't have anything to eat from very early in the morning until late evening, for that reason she arranged with the new cleaning lady to feed us at around 5pm.

Peter smoked awful smelly cigars, and the cleaning lady removed the offensive cigarette butts every afternoon; until she arrived, the house stank of a rancid, penetrating, foul smell.

There was something wrong with Marcella by the middle of the week. She was agitated; her bad temper was evident and she began to leave angry messages on her mother's cellular phone.

Her mother returned Marcella's first call and immediately realized that an argument was brewing; the reason appeared to be related to the money Marcella had given her during the previous ten weeks.

Marcella was reassured that she would receive whatever cash was left after the cleaner was paid; her mother made her intention clear, however, she sensed Marcella as usual, and for an unknown reason, was already working on an argument, therefore, she decided not to return any more of her phone calls. As the days passed by every message left was more aggressive, more abusive and angrier. Marcella wasn't able to contain her ferocious rage.

Meanwhile the situation at home was unpleasant, Peter wasn't friendly to us, and Marcella's agitation was disturbing.

It was Saturday morning. Marcella was extremely tense and agitated. We went downstairs and waited anxiously for our parents return.

They had decided to cut the holiday short in view that Marcella's birthday was on Sunday. They arrived after lunch and the argument was waiting for them, no soon had they entered the house when Marcella began to ask her mother for the cash she had given her, and demanded that she give it back immediately. It was a scene like in the movies we watched on television. The abuse and loud screams from Marcella were absolutely out of place, her screams and uncontrolled anger made us run away to hide.

Although a Saturday, and the shop wasn't open, Peter left for the day before our parents arrived. His stinking cigarette butts in the kitchen waste bin were left behind as well as the horrid smell; unfortunately, the cleaning lady didn't visit home the previous afternoon to empty the bin.

Marcella's mother asked why Peter took the liberty of smoking inside the house, when he knew perfectly well that they didn't smoke. The only answer she received was in the form of screams and abuse from Marcella.

I was sorry for them, felt powerless to do anything and wished I could've warned them. Finally, the screams stopped and Marcella's parents gave her the gift they had bought for her birthday, a beautiful blue pacific pearl with a little diamond which she threw aside and said, 'thanks'.

She didn't ask if they had a good holiday either. She also received half the amount of money she had given her mother which was the amount left after the cleaner was paid. It was fair, since we were her responsibility.

The rest of the afternoon was unpleasant to say the least. She remained in her room, didn't talk at all, and only appeared during dinner time; she sat in complete silence, consumed her food and left the table.

Their holiday was totally ruined and the bit of relaxation found on previous days had been erased within a few minutes.

We didn't know what Marcella's plans were, but she had certainly prepared one of her biggest and most malicious performances to date.

The next day she packed her bags and left around 11am without saying a word to her parents. She did say good bye to us, by then we felt lost. She was going with Peter, he had organized a trip around the world and that was very important to her, her parents feelings weren't taken into consideration. Her behaviour was truly appalling.

We felt very sorry about what happened, but without knowledge of the past we couldn't understand the present situation.

Her parents were terribly upset and very hurt by Marcella's behaviour, these incidents always caught them by surprise; invariably, events of this type without failure occurred after a brief period of peace and tranquillity, when they had built the hope that Marcella's attitude towards them might've changed, but every time their hopes were totally annihilated.

Marcella was like a mythical dragon who threw fire at the most unexpected moment and for no logical reason.

Mia and I were affected by it too, but sometimes the feline intuition tells you that certain things do not change, and we felines accept the situation or move away. In this case we knew that Marcella had met her match, a person very much like her, someone who possessed an abrupt and sour manner. What a shame we thought.

All the goodness her parents had tried to infuse into her soul would vanish within a short period of time, and we wouldn't be able to recognize the lovely girl who grew up with so much love and care.

Marcella was away with Peter, and whether she cared about the emotional destruction she left at the time of her departure, we will never know. She left with the knowledge that her parent's short holiday was absolutely ruined, and the week they had managed to steal from their work had been totally wasted.

CHAPTER 6

Marcella's mother's illness started with a cough and a blocked nose, soon it developed into a deep chest infection; she took antibiotics but the fever due to the lung infection was almost constant, sometimes she went to bed with an elevated temperature, and we tried to nurse her by laying next to her, with the idea to help her recover, but she used to get hotter and couldn't sleep. At times I used to put my head really close to her neck hoping that my best energies would pass to her, and thus help to accelerate her recovery.

Her work load was immense, she worked all day and tried to sleep during the night with both of us by her side; she was our mum and we were very worried, so was our dad.

She coughed continuously; the cough appeared to come from her stomach and made her very sick. We knew it was more than a physical illness, the symptoms were caused by emotional distress and grief, but sometimes the feline language doesn't translate clearly and the information is not passed on successfully.

We purred and lovingly looked after her, but her health didn't improve for a long time. She did a lot of thinking while

Marcella was away. She brought to the conscious mind memories stored throughout the years, and also read the notes she'd taken every time a horrible situation had occurred.

She studied and analysed Marcella's behavioural pattern throughout the many times when Marcella was unbearable, and obnoxious, and she used to tell her not to push her luck too far, because as much as she loved her, one day she could become tired of her bad manner and hostility towards them, and when that moment arrived there wouldn't be any turning back. Figuratively, she used to say: 'all the bolts and locks on the door will be firmly closed'.

She was unable to understand Marcella's obscure reasons for her display of intense dislike and anger towards them. Once Marcella became an adult, and was free from her biological father's negative influence, the logical outcome would've been a change for the better because she was a good daughter, a girl with a good heart and in addition she had many positive qualities; not only these elements were present, but the parent daughter relationship had been a happy and harmonious one, perhaps ideal, because it was more like a fond friendship with a deep closeness.

Unfortunately, the changes expected didn't eventuate, and Marcella was determined to upset everybody, including herself using the same tactics she had used as a child.

Why was it so? Why to be so destructive when she had a comfortable, stable home where she was treated well and with love. Could it be that her biological father's destructive programming had continued to exert such power and influence over her, after twenty three years?

She behaved exactly in the same manner when she was twelve years old; it was at that time, when her biological father instructed her to make her parents life as unbearable as possible.

It appeared to be that Marcella's purpose in life was to destroy her parents' relationship.

Marcella, at the age of twelve, sadly commenced her metamorphosis from a loving, happy girl into a difficult person with destructive characteristics similar to her biological father.

Was her behaviour inherited in the same way she had inherited his dark hair? Had his genetic material taken over to the point that it was possible to discard a good upbringing, or was her terrible manner a by-product of his malicious mind, that during the crucial development years had interfered with her well balanced emotional conscience?

She demonstrated an incredible anger, and a destructive, uncontrolled dislike almost bordering on hate towards her parents. She argued at any moment, and for the most unexpected of reasons, she wasn't capable of a normal discussion to resolve whatever differences of opinion she had. It was distressing for everybody.

At the onset of those disturbing characteristics, her parents believed it was part of the normal transition to her teen years aggravated by the conflict her father created, and as she grew older, she'd grow out of it.

There was no apparent reason for that behaviour to continue after she decided that her biological father didn't deserve her efforts.

She was an adult who thought clearly at times in reference to her biological father treatment of her; the bad influence he had on her, and some of the consequences of that influence, such as the effect on her selection of men; she had realized that unwillingly, she selected individuals that behaved towards her in a similar manner to her biological father.

She was logical and sensible on her assessment about her biological father's obnoxious and destructive behaviour towards her and her mother. She also recognized the problems her mother had while she was married to him, and she expressed it without anger or resentment.

Sometimes she openly said that in her opinion he was so awful, she believed her mother had made the correct decision to leave him, and at the same time wondered how she had managed to live with him for nearly eight years.

At the end, after all the soul searching there was no answer to the current situation.

Her parents thought there were left with two avenues of choice; try to reason with Marcella in relation to her outrageous behaviour, that was almost an impossible task, because of her aggressive manner every time something of this nature was discussed; or simply wait to see if a change appeared in the near future that indicated she was sorry for the unnecessary hurt and stress caused.

Perhaps the new relationship with Peter would bring some positive outcome that could modify her behavioural pattern, after all, she was thirty three years old, and if in the past she had any fear of abandonment from her parents, now that she had a relationship of her own perhaps her fears would ease.

Her current behaviour didn't appear to be positive in any way. Many times in the past when Marcella's mother was terribly upset due to Marcella's usual carry on, she used to say: 'remember my philosophy on life Marcella. I have, like everybody else, the capacity to forgive, but at certain point when that capacity has reached its limit there is no return, no matter who it may be. I firmly believe that a relationship should bring love and mutual respect, when those very important elements are missing there is no point pretending that a relationship exists. You know that I never argue, and I never offer reasons for my detachment'.

'The one who causes me anguish and pain will find that the door will close, the ground will freeze, and an invisible barrier which stops access to my soul and my love will appear. As you have observed, those who have upset me to the extreme and made me reach the limit of my capacity to forgive, have already found themselves in a situation from which there is no possible return into my life'.

'My patience is finite, do not push you luck, because as much as I love you, if your behaviour continues to be so incredibly destructive towards us, if your intended purpose is to destroy our relationship, the final outcome will not be related to how much we love and care for you, it will be our self preservation'.

At the time Marcella didn't respond, so we don't know what her thoughts were. She appeared to be totally dislocated from the situation.

We received a postcard, and after eight or nine weeks Marcella called her mother to say she had returned from her trip, and would come home in a couple of days; her parents had made the very hard decision to distance themselves from Marcella. If she was away from them, perhaps she would begin to think about them differently, and perhaps would start to realize that her bad manner towards them was an oddity, something abnormal between parent and daughter, and she may appreciate that she was loved.

From a feline point of view, it would have been a struggle for all of us to continue the acceptance of her obnoxious and hostile behaviour, as well as the continuous conflict she was capable of bringing into our lives.

Although her argumentative manner wasn't directed to Mia and me, we also suffered the consequence of that stress. I used to curl up in a little ball and tried to sleep through the stress, but Mia threw up constantly.

At the same time it was a struggle not to take her once more, and continue to hope that perhaps she would change in the near future. Marcella was thirty three years old; how many more years did we have to wait to see a change? The decision was made, because there wasn't any other choice available.

Marcella's mother said: 'Marcella, stay where you are'.

It was very hard for her mother to say it, but Marcella hadn't left any other option. If she valued the relationship with them, she would have to rectify and make good the errors of the past.

Her parents didn't expect many positive changes which seems a bit negative, but after so many incidents in the past when they truly had hoped to see a small sign of improvement, and their expectations had been obliterated, they thought she would carry on as usual, as if nothing had happened, and in the same way she had always pretended not to care.

It was matter of wait, see and trust that Marcella had finally understood she had pushed them too far. It was a very uncharacteristic response from their otherwise loving, and caring manner, always ready to embrace her, resolve her grievances and give her love.

Marcella's parents believed she needed a bit a of a shake up to make her realize it wasn't fair to continue pretending that every time an outburst of obnoxious, cruel behaviour occurred towards them, the end result would be the same as if nothing had happened. She perhaps would be able to pretend that nothing had happened. Turn around and expect that everything would be as it had been many times in the past, when she had behaved badly and after a couple of days everything had returned to normality.

This time the pain she caused was very intense, and all that was needed from Marcella was a sincere apology for her wrong and insensitive behaviour; a couple of honest loving words would have fixed everything.

It was Saturday. A week after they had arrived from their holiday. Marcella arrived with Peter who said he was madly in love with her and wanted to marry her.

Her mother's response to Peter was: 'do not make her a bitter person, she is a good girl'. 'We have given her lots of love and care'.

'Oh, yes I will look after her', was his response.

We didn't see Marcella very often after her return; she came to visit on a Saturday or Sunday, Peter was always with her. As much as we loved Marcella we felt detached from her, and experienced the feeling that perhaps she didn't love us anymore. For these two felines life couldn't get any better, we lived in a palace, felt loved and we were much pampered.

Winter arrived and our parents always went to the mountains for their mid-year ski holiday; it was arranged with Marcella that she would look after us for eight days, but she didn't want to come to our home, she instead preferred us to come to live with her and Peter in their city apartment, not for a week but permanently. Marcella didn't make her intentions clear otherwise, her parents would've organized a house sitter they knew well.

Peter and Marcella arrived to pick us up, collected our favourite blankets and toys and we left. From the first moment after we arrived at their little apartment we realized we weren't wanted.

What a miserable week we had, Peter was annoyed with me because I was unhappy and couldn't sleep, I just wanted to return home; I howled, scratched the carpet, and the entry door, I also tried to run away. Poor Mia was under the bed petrified, due to the different noises we heard. There were no trees or birds to watch, and the days passed by very slowly and sad. We were alone most of the day and nobody explained the noises.

We wanted our parents back.

I heard a telephone conversation Marcella had with her mother. Marcella said: 'they are fine; you shouldn't come here because you will disturb them'. I said to myself: I bet she is terribly upset and misses us; probably she has tears in her eyes.

My heart sank, our life once more was miserable; Peter hit my bum several times to stop me from howling. I suffered the pain; it only encouraged me to continue. I howled louder. I knew that it would be the only way we would get out of there. I told Mia to howl and run up and down the length of the narrow corridor to drive them crazy.

Marcella constantly said to Peter that we would get used to it and to be patient; the more she said things like that, the more we howled and the more Mia ran up and down along the corridor. I even tried to escape when the door was open for a brief moment.

Marcella's mother called again, and I could determine from Marcella's responses that her mother was concerned about our wellbeing. Marcella said: 'they are fine and I do not want you to see them'.

That night I said to Mia: you must join me to howl as loud as you can, you must scratch the carpet and run like a maniac the length of the corridor, we must get out of here as fast as possible, we can't get used to this place, if we don't force our way out of here, we will be trapped, and our life will be very sad, like it was before our parents took care of us.

We were terribly nervous that evening, we could hardly eat our dinner, and Mia threw up the couple of morsels she ate; as soon as they turned the lights off and went to bed, we began to howl, we ran the length of the corridor and we both scratched the entry door, we were desperate to get out of there, Peter got up and hit my bum several times; his actions turned me into a truly savage feline.

From that moment I was no longer the gentle feline Franc, as he came close to me I stretched my claws with the intent to shred his skin, and I showed him my canines like a wild beast. I wasn't aware that within me existed such aggression.

I also encouraged Mia to growl at him. Our determination to leave that place had to bear some reward. Mia and I growled as loud as possible and showed our teeth most of the night.

The next day without any explanation we were put into the cages for transportation and went straight home; we arrived at around 10am we had been terribly missed.

We were exhausted by the lack of sleep, we had lost weight, our coat had lost its shine, and the skin was dry and flaky due to the stress we had experienced. Mia was sick with fear and she threw up constantly; we had spent ten horrible days with Marcella and Peter at their little and noisy, city apartment.

We had tuna for lunch and went to bed; the ordeal had a happy ending for us.

CHAPTER 7

Marcella's sporadic visits always happened in Peter's company; they arrived home on their way to see friends or after they had been somewhere. Not once did she bother to visit her parents on her own. Peter's unfriendly and hostile manner, together with his presence was an impediment to have a good, deep conversation with her parents, and therefore, nothing was discussed about her odd manner towards them; or was it Peter who tried to isolate her from our family? She never addressed the issue either when she talked to her mother on the phone.

At the sound of Peter and Marcella's voices we ran and hid, and the times they came through the door we had the fear of being taken away, fortunately their visits were infrequent. Sometimes we didn't come out at all to say hello, when we heard that they were leaving, we cautiously walked out of our hiding places, and Marcella used to say: 'so you are here, where were you?'

Life returned to normality for us, and after a brief period of time our ordeal was forgotten, once more, we began to enjoy our surroundings with great delight; that was the time when our parents began to talk about the history of Marcella's hostile behaviour. It was long and complicated. They often referred to the incredible anguish her behavior brought throughout the years. They weren't certain when or why it all began.

Her personality suffered a dramatic change. She had been a lovely, happy, popular girl, until she became involved with a school group that seemed to encourage her to be the silly dunce of the class, as a result her lack of interest in her academic studies surfaced, and this appeared to be considered a success, because it made her friends laugh.

Perhaps we could go further back in time they used to say. I just sat on my little blanket by the window, listened to their conversations, and I relied on my ability to preserve the knowledge word by word, with the intention to write the story at the appropriate moment.

Marcella's mother and biological father divorced when she was nearly eight years old, it was a very acrimonious divorce. Marcella's father despite being an older man lost the plot, just because his young wife decided to terminate an unhappy marriage. The marriage had been a very unhappy one from the very beginning. Marcella's biological father was about to marry someone else, but he was taken by Marcella's mother's beauty, and decided to drop his fiancé basically, at the church threshold. Apparently the wedding date had been determined, and the invitations had been distributed.

Marcella's mother was younger than him by about thirteen years, she was vivacious and with an outgoing personality, although, rather reserved which seems a contradiction; a very artistic person, with a sensitive personality, yet determined, and tenacious.

From the onset of their marriage they had constant arguments about almost everything; the disagreements, criticism, and disinterest from his part were a very sore point and she was constantly upset. He, continuously, from the beginning of the marriage, and every time he had the opportunity, humiliated and ridiculed her at home, as well as in the presence of other people. His manner gave the impression that he sought for a chance to destroy her personality in front of strangers or friends.

At home, after returning from work she was just the beast of burden who carried out all the domestic chores, and looked after Marcella with not a bit of help from him.

She began to tell one of many terribly sad episodes that occurred while married to him, she would have been about twenty four years old; she had developed a tremendous stomach ache, and although, she had visited the general practitioner on several occasions no diagnosis was offered.

It was mid afternoon on a Sunday when the acute pain developed and she went to bed; it was about 6pm when she had to get up to prepare some food for Marcella because her husband refused to do it. In his opinion he didn't marry to cook or clean; after she prepared a light meal for Marcella she returned to bed feeling unwell.

He, at about 8pm asked her if she wasn't going to prepare his dinner; after that he prepared some food just for himself.

She then said to him: 'I have to eat something otherwise I would feel worse tomorrow'. His response was: 'sick people don't eat'.

The following day she visited a new general practitioner, who said she had to go to hospital for an emergency appendix operation, otherwise it could rupture.

This was one of the many unpleasant events in her daily life while she was married to Marcella's biological father. Life was dreary indeed; no matter what she did her unhappiness was overwhelming.

He used to taunt her saying she was ugly, and fat, when the reality was that she had become skin and bones, almost anorexic.

A change began to develop after some friends of his arrived for afternoon tea on a Sunday; it was a summer afternoon and she wore a skimpy little dress which showed her fragile frame. His friend's wife, Luisa, observed her skeletal appearance and made the comment that a beautiful girl like her should take more care of her appearance.

She, for the first time was able to tell someone the reality of her life. The woman, in her forties, was appalled as she listened carefully. Offered valuable advice which she put into practice, and in this way she began to restore her lost self confidence.

Many times she warned him that his manner wasn't tolerable and one day she would leave him. His immediate response was to tell her: 'leave, and as you leave take your daughter and give me ten thousand dollars for having put up with you'.

'The day for me to leave is drawing closer and closer, so when it arrives, try not to appear as a victim', used to be her response.

His lack of interest in Marcella also created a great rift with the child; every time she spent time with him, the arguments were phenomenal, not even a brief moment in the children's section at the park was exempt, Marcella normally returned home screaming and shouting 'I hate him, I hate him'

When he was asked to explain the reason for Marcella's reaction, he without failure blamed her for the altercation; either Marcella was difficult or had a bad temper.

She is only a six years old child and you are an old man, her mother used to say. He was antagonistic, and the constant animosity created a dreadful atmosphere to live in; not only negative for a child's development, but also for her wellbeing, and the wellbeing of her mother, who sometimes thought it would be better to die, than to continue to live under the daily emotional conflict and misery.

For the sake of Marcella she continued to struggle with the hope that one day her life would take a turn for the better, and a more harmonious relationship would come to her.

She thought of leaving him many times, once when the infant was just two months old, and she realized there wouldn't be a future with the man; she packed her belongings, the baby and called a taxi, while she waited for the taxi somehow her mother arrived, and convinced her to stay with her husband.

Time showed it was a great mistake to listen to her mother, life didn't improve at all, every day of her life was shrouded with unhappiness, and for nearly eight years she suffocated while tried to stay alive for her child; in many occasions she wanted to end it all, but the love for Marcella and a little ray of optimism maintained her strength. Consequently, the constant thought of finding a way to leave him dominated her life.

She matured and after close to eight years of utter misery, she couldn't take it anymore; that was when she decided to leave him. The situation was tense. As he realized that it was final, he offered that he could change. Apparently, the idea that he could've changed was instigated after a brief visit to his sister's home somewhere in Germany.

During the visit, his sister's husband complained about her argumentative and antagonistic behaviour, as well as the total lack of emotional interest in the children and him; his sister's husband said: 'I've given her an ultimatum, either she modifies her behaviour or I leave within the next six months, I can't tolerate this anymore; I think six years of a cold, and an emotional dead marriage are enough'. He then realized that his complaints were of the same nature of his wife's complaints, and after his return decided that if she continued to show discontent, he could change.

Her reply was: 'Too late! You have reached the limit of what I can endure, I've given you nearly eight years of my precious life; you don't deserve a fraction of a second more'. With this response she began divorce proceedings.

The home situation became quite tense when he realized that there was a new man on her horizon, and it was even worse when they decided to marry as soon as the divorce was obtained.

Marcella's biological father's revenge was to turn the child against her mother, and the new man in her life. He did everything within his reach to achieve his goal. During the divorce proceeding he accused Marcella's mother of being a prostitute, the judge was quite severe, and demanded he present proof; that demand silenced him, but a new tactic to disrupt life developed.

He began to tell Marcella to lie to her mother, and that her new husband would rape her. The manner, in which he said it, was enough to disturb Marcella deeply. Fortunately, she didn't understand the word rape, and he didn't explain it either, but told her that it was something really awful. Also he told her that she would be abandoned one day, because her mother didn't want her, and didn't love her. If she loved you, your mother would've continued to live with me.

The Social Workers promptly put an end to that lunacy, but a rift caused by the anxiety had started to take hold, and Marcella was greatly affected. Her studies suffered from an early age, her behaviour was erratic since she was told to lie and deceive. Her biological father created an anxiety problem in her, by constantly telling her that her mother didn't want her, and she could get rid of her when she least expected.

The designated days for him to pick her up from her place of residence were marked with disappointment and frustration, because he didn't turn up, or arrived two or more hours later than the agreed time.

Marcella would wait for several hours; an eternity for an eight years old child, therefore, by the time he arrived she was anxious, angry, and her behaviour was obnoxious towards him initially, and when she returned home towards her parents. Also the situation was aggravated by the fact that often after he picked her up, he dropped her at some friend's house and left her there for the rest of the day; he turned up to collect her a short time before he had to bring her home, and thus aggravated Marcella's already disturbed emotions.

Unfortunately, Marcella didn't discuss the situation at the time when it was happening; she only talked about it some years later.

During the period of time when she was left at his friends' place, people asked questions about her new life, where they lived, about her mother, and whether it was true she went out frequently with many men; that only increased her level of anxiety. To make matters worse, if her biological father was present, he answered the questions before Marcella could reply.

The place where she lived was a dump, she had useless cats instead of a dog, and the new school wasn't as prestigious as the one she used to attend before the divorce; it was normally followed by a myriad of false, mean accusations against her mother being a call girl, and the rape possibility the child may experience by the mother's new husband. It was terribly upsetting for her.

On most occasions Marcella returned home emotionally disturbed, and as soon as she entered the house, she broke into tears and screamed that she hated him. He is mean, and really nasty, she used to say.

Marcella's parents had the daunting task of repairing the anxiety, and the insecurities that had been implanted in her by her biological father during a very destructive couple of hours. It took them several days to dissipate her troubled emotions, they had to work hard to bring her to normality; unfortunately the same scene would be repeated time and time again.

The only alternative would have been to go to court once more; more cost, more disturbances for everybody and the end result quite likely would have been one more of frustration towards an impractical law of shared responsibility, without taking into consideration the harmful situation that had been created. The god like manner in which the decisions are made is totally unfair.

The school principal was aware of the problem and she tried to help; she was the person who saw at first hand the changes after Marcella's biological father had access. She was patient and understanding; sometimes she called Marcella's mother to ask if Marcella had seen her father.

She wanted to be sure that she had seen her father the previous weekend, because the child was in a terrible and agitated emotional condition and she didn't want to punish her unfairly. Without failure every time the school principal called, it had been the case.

A very aggravating situation for Marcella was the knowledge that her biological father didn't want to contribute to the cost of her education. He never paid school fees or any other expenses; he reluctantly contributed, after a court order garnished his wages for the minimum amount anybody could give his own child. She was resentful of his lack of interest not only financially, but emotionally as well.

Little Marcella was placed in a very difficult situation for a child. She was used by her biological father as a missile with the intention of derailing her mother's new life.

Marcella didn't sleep well, refused to eat, she was absent minded at school, irritable and argumentative at home, couldn't concentrate to do her homework; she showed all the symptoms of acute stress.

Her biological father consciously tormented her life, for no other purpose than to satisfy his own inadequacies, by blaming someone else for his problems.

While sitting on my little blanket, I heard the recollection about a wonderful holiday the family had sometime before my sister Mia and I arrived into their lives. They went on a four weeks holiday. They drove across the semi-deserted land, saw many towns and arrived at a place by the sea where they spent a week, then returned through a different route where they saw other places of interest.

Marcella was happy, enjoyed life, was interested in all the activities pursued, and at no time there was any problematic behaviour; her biological father was never mentioned and the holiday was truly happy for everybody.

The following week after their return home from the holiday, Marcella saw her father, when she left home she was a happy, little girl, she had stories to tell, she even brought him a souvenir; by the time she returned home late that afternoon, she was agitated, stressed, and deeply disturbed. Didn't talk about what happened during the day. She only said 'I hate him. He humiliated me in front of those awful people, his friends. He said all those awful things, he always says'.

Whatever her parents did to restore the child's happiness, their efforts were always derailed by a miserable human being more interested in creating havoc and destruction. It was a battle against a spiteful and sinister person.

It was a personal vendetta and the results of his actions would affect his own daughter for the rest of her life.

Marcella's biological father's stupidity and selfishness was of such magnitude, that he chose to be blind to the damage his actions would bring to her personal development. It would affect her future relationships, her emotional wellbeing, and her studies.

He perhaps thought that if he managed to alter Marcella's behaviour, her mother's new relationship would fail, and that would be the real proof that he wasn't the one with the problem, it was someone else's.

I sat on my little blanket which had been placed in the sun, I listened carefully to everything and took notes, I also placed strict attention to the chronological aspects of the story, because I was certain that one day it would fall on my shoulders to tell the sequence of events in an unbiased and accurate manner, not just for my own peace of mind, but also to tell a tale of unusual circumstances, and such unexpected turn of events, that not even the most competent clairvoyant would have been able to foretell.

The subject about Marcella's behaviour was raised time and time again; her parents searched for answers, and tried to understand her erratic and destructive manner towards them as well as her own self.

This feline observed that she behaved in a way as if there wasn't any love for them and wanted them to be unhappy.

From her early teens when all the conflict began to emerge, Marcella did everything within her power to create animosity and antagonism, when she succeeded, and her parents disagreed on simple matters, by the time she turned her back she had a smirk of accomplishment on her face, and went to her bedroom leaving her parents debating whatever just happened.

The pattern had existed since she was a child, and at the age of thirty three the unusual manner still had a hold on her life.

Her mother tried to look for assistance, and had several sessions with a sociologist during the first year of Marcella's college; Marcella had some sessions as well, but she refused to continue with the treatment due to a tremendous dislike towards the professional.

The sociologist findings were sketchy since not enough information had been collected; although the result was inconclusive something surfaced, which was an absolute puzzle to Marcella's parents; her behaviour was premeditated, and all her performances were planned to create disruption, anguish, and conflict.

They couldn't understand why Marcella's final purpose was to create conflict; with an inconclusive result, there was no opportunity to find the deeper reasons that affected her personality. Her parents were certain that the biological father was the cause of many of her problems.

It was a destructive path, even for Marcella, because she became so worked up about what was going to upset her parents, that it also affected her life immensely. There were the moods swings, anger, and some form of phobia towards a peaceful and tranquil environment.

Her objective consumed her; she also gave free reign to a very argumentative nature. A combination of all those aspects indicated there was a possibility she was using drugs, since this is apparently the characteristic behaviour pattern of individuals that consume mind altering substances.

Her parents chose to believe that it wasn't the case; it was too ugly to contemplate that the person they loved and cared for was destroying her life, and in the process would hurt them.

The sadness of it all was that the current manner wasn't a pattern Marcella had fallen into within the last years, it had occurred for a long period of time; almost since she was twelve years old. Every holiday was marked with a horrendous argument, Marcella was unhappy and argumentative whether she was taken on holiday or not.

On several occasions they were in the car going somewhere for a long weekend while Marcella carried on with her antics. Her parents patiently tried to resolve the issue, but at the end it was so incredibly unpleasant that they returned home before they arrived to the city outskirts.

To find relief from Marcella's poisonous behaviour, after Marcella reached the age of twelve, sporadically, she was sent to stay with her biological father just for a weekend. It was a real problem as well, the tears, the screams, because it was boring to stay with him and she didn't get along with him either. She returned home with a myriad of complaints and always made the point to say that she hated him, she cried, and therefore, her parent's rest was ruined; it didn't matter what option they took, it brought invariably the same result.

The other problem was that Marcella saw her father infrequently, and after a period of stability at home, the mere fact that during a few hours her father was able to create such level of anxiety in her, was disturbing for everybody.

On the other hand it was impossible to know what he said to her during those hours that created the disturbance, it was rather difficult to ascertain whether it was an overreaction on her part so she could call more attention when with her biological father or at home.

The only certainty her parents had, was that after Marcella saw her biological father she was absolutely unbearable for approximately a week; the impact was so severe that many times they wished, she could understand he was the source of her unhappiness, and therefore make the decision to stop seeing him as the child counsellor had indicated four years before.

Marcella was fifteen. It was then when her biological father decided to re-marry and for that reason stopped seeing her. He never contacted her to make her aware of his decision;

Marcella only found out that he intended not to see her again after a telephone conversation. According to Marcella, her biological father's new wife prohibited him to make contact with her, due to the fact that she considered Marcella to be a very disruptive and malevolent person, who would end up destroying their marriage.

Marcella then took a severe dislike to the woman; she was just a peasant who couldn't speak English or her native Spanish at all, she was ugly, common, uneducated, and she looked like a ball of lard. In addition she had appalling manners.

Her parents listened with amusement at Marcella's reaction, and responded that if the woman was so horrid, first, her father deserved someone horrid to share his horrid personality; second, perhaps the woman would stop him from tormenting her, and maybe if she didn't see him anymore, her life will be better without him after all.

'Probably some years into the future you will end up being very grateful and thanking the woman for the outcome'.

Marcella didn't give up and decided to contact her father at his place of work; she began to see him sporadically at lunch time during his break. Marcella was attending high school, and at the time asked for permission to leave school to have lunch with her biological father, she told the teacher that her mother was aware of it, which wasn't the case. This was one of many situations created to disrupt and antagonize, and her biological father was a willing participant.

Marcella's parents noticed at the time, certain nervousness in her demeanour, and she was also terribly unsettled; didn't sleep well, was extremely argumentative, angry and edgy. Unfortunately this manner is sometimes typical during the teenage years, consequently, they tried to be flexible and understanding; their main priority was to treat Marcella as a friend, and to show support and patience while the circumstances were difficult.

They wanted to preserve the good relationship that already existed, she, at times communicated well, expressed her anxieties, and they took those moments as a positive outcome to an otherwise complex situation.

Marcella's mother left work early and on her way home, saw Marcella walking along the road well before school had finished for the day. She arrived home and waited for Marcella who arrived some minutes later. This unexpected event gave her the opportunity to ask questions. Once Marcella realized she had been caught, there was an element of relief to her conscience for her foolishness.

Her mother asked for a reason to carry on like that, after all, her biological father very clearly, didn't want to see her, and when he saw her, he affected her emotionally with his cruel, distant and uninterested manner. Marcella's response was that it wasn't him who didn't want to see her, it was an imposition the horrid woman forced upon him, and of course, she was who stopped him.

Her parents contacted school and made the teacher aware of the situation.

This new approach to see him didn't improve the relationship at all; in many instances she would call her mother as soon as she parted company with her biological father, and confided that he was so awful she wouldn't see him again.

Apparently, the common practice of his to humiliate Marcella in front of people she didn't even know, by saying unsavoury assumptions about her mother, had continued seven years after their divorce.

Marcella was asked: 'why were you with him? Why do you continue to leave school to expose yourself to the same routine, time after time?'

The response was: 'Oh, I thought he would behave differently today'. Those episodes were a constant source of grief to Marcella, and often she asked for advice. The obvious answer couldn't be said, unfortunately, her parents were caught in a dilemma; if they said to Marcella do not see your biological father again, perhaps they would be blamed for the advice given.

It would have been the correct thing to say taking into consideration the disruption and unhappiness caused to Marcella, but her parents always responded: 'you must make that decision yourself, he is the type of person we would've sent to hell, long time ago, because he is a destructive and mean person; we observe your frustration and the anxiety he implants every time you see him'.

'We can't tell you what to do; whatever you decide, it will happen when you are ready'.

I am a happy feline, I have my sister Mia, I am loved and I love my family. This is a story without a happy ending I used to think as I listened. I felt extremely fortunate that Mia and I ended up with our new parents, all our struggles had been compensated and our life was secure and happy.

I deeply wished that Marcella could appreciate the good parents she also had. For these many reasons I continue to tell this tale with the sincere hope that we may see a change in the near future.

Marcella's was still at school when her parents decided to create some extra activities which would involve spending more time with her, in that way she would have to engage with them in different environments during activities that perhaps she would enjoy, and would help to alleviate her lack of communication, and also may mitigate her anxieties. It was a way of showing how much they loved her and cared for her.

Her mother organized flamenco dancing lessons, there were girls of different ages in the class, and the fact that mother and daughter attended the classes together, was a special event within the group. Marcella was well liked and soon they began to attend classes twice a week; it was absolutely enjoyable for both of them. Marcella, with her great musical ear was better than her mother, and soon learnt the difficult steps which she performed with great dexterity; it was something totally different and certainly would provide Marcella with a new hobby.

The flamenco teacher organized activities which involved the entire group. They provided entertainment during special celebrations, such as International Women's Day, and similar occasions. Everybody looked forward to those performances; Marcella had costumes made and the activity created an extra connection with her mother. The flamenco classes continued for approximately four years until the teacher left, and the group disintegrated.

Her father bought a small two men sailing dinghy. Marcella attended sailing classes, and they began to sail during Sunday competitions the sailing club organized. She enjoyed the races, but didn't want to mix with the rest of the competitors and they both returned home. Sometimes she was a bit more amiable and talked to some guys who participated in the contest.

She obviously had fun and enjoyed talking about the experiences which happened during the racing competition; she laughed describing the times when the boat over-turned and she was under the vessel, it appears that she truly enjoyed those moments. They sailed during the summer season, but didn't want to continue with the sailing competitions; she complained about the aggression the participants exhibited while on the water.

Marcella's behaviour began to show some improvement; the last years of high school were certainly more pleasant for the entire family, the biggest disturbances arose after the occasions she had seen her father.

High school finished, and her results weren't the best, but her parents were happy that she managed to persevere under the emotional stress her biological father so cruelly imposed on her. Fortunately, her college entry would depend on an ability test more than the final year results.

Marcella's emotional struggles were present for many more years; she continued to see her biological father with less frequency, and that helped restore her emotional strength and balance, but then she felt guilty that the contact was kept to a minimum, and consequently organized to meet him.

He never called to make any arrangements to see her; it was she who organized when to see him. As a consequence of his treatment of her, the emotional rollercoaster continued throughout her college days and of course that contributed to the disaster she faced after her first year of college.

Her great dream and ambition was to become a fashion designer; her abilities were so natural, her parents believed it would've been a breeze for her from the beginning of the course to graduation. They were totally wrong.

They didn't for a second imagined that Marcella's talents would be wasted, just because of a bad attitude and a lack of interest in her studies. It was unbelievable to see her disinterest in something that had been her dream since she was a child.

The first year of college ended, and Marcella had to carry one subject, for the rest of the following year to be able to progress to her second year. At the end of the second year she failed the subject and she was refused entry to the college.

Sometimes Marcella's parents talked about the negative input her father had on all aspects of her life including her studies. Even Marcella was perplexed when her father said to her that education didn't mean anything, and that the fact that anybody had a piece of paper with a name written on it wasn't a warranty for a good life. Difficult to believe those words were said by a qualified engineer to his college student daughter.

She found herself without a college placement. Her parents knew the cause of her problems and offered a solution.

She could matriculate in a college of her choice; they would pay for the fees and materials required for her studies, they would also provide the cost of transport from home to college, and the return home and nothing else. She had to prepare food at home for her lunch, and no more pocket money would be given until she finished her course and received a certificate.

If she failed once more, there would be no more money for another course no matter what. She would have to work to pay for any further studies if she decided to achieve something, or make the choice to work as an unskilled person; it was entirely up to her and they wouldn't say anything anymore. This was her last opportunity and it was up to her to take it or leave it.

To her parent's surprise, she applied herself as she had never done before; they never had to ask if her assignments had been completed; didn't go out at all, and she studied with enormous dedication for the entire year with the bad luck that her course was discontinued, and she had to matriculate in another college to start all over again. It would be her fourth year without achieving anything.

Her parents accepted the situation and financed her studies for a further two years. It was an inferior course, she wouldn't be a designer as she had always dreamt; her studies would qualify her to be a pattern maker, and general factory assistant for all the related areas of clothing manufacture.

She was encouraged to achieve her dreams, they tried to make her see that perhaps it was a blessing in disguise the fact that she had to learn how to construct garments; it would be an asset to be able to know how everything is put together after the initial design. She could have progressed from there if she had worked harder to achieve her dream, but she didn't.

Marcella showed a lot of initiative during that period, she found jobs during the holidays, worked on the weekends for pocket money and often requested that her parents visit the shop where she worked.

It was a period of great improvement and harmony for the entire family; there were short lived moments of anxiety after she saw her biological father, but it appeared not to affect her with the same intensity.

Her mother also found ways to engage her in other activities as well, not only to further develop their relationship, but to demonstrate that any person that wants to succeed, has to invest a great deal of effort, positive thinking, tenacity, and commitment to be able to reach a positive result.

A lecture about Coco Chanel was advertised at one of the museums, and she booked two places. Such an interesting subject for an aspiring designer her mother thought, it was an excellent opportunity for Marcella to learn about a life that showed such talent and vision. Coco Chanel lived throughout a period in history that was quite restrictive for females who wanted to achieve their ambitions and fulfil their dreams.

The lecture was very comprehensive and it took the entire day. There were early films which presented her life story, and later films which showed the style history of the garments at the moment of her design development. It clearly demonstrated and underlined the struggles and difficulties she encountered to be accepted. There were several authentic Chanel garments on display, and one of the organizers described the construction methods that existed before Chanel transformed the female fashion, and the success she achieved through hard work and dedication. Apparently, Chanel thought that at the time women outfits made them look like meringues.

It was a fabulous lecture, very entertaining, informative and most of all, it left the feeling that everything is possible through dedication, and enthusiasm.

From Marcella's point of view it was boring; the women who organized the event had fat legs and their appearance was somehow disgustingly ordinary.

Marcella, her mother told her, 'we came here to learn about Coco Chanel, we didn't come here to praise or criticize the women who presented the lecture, so what if their legs are fat, they have a good knowledge of the subject and that is what really counts'.

Marcella didn't want to discuss it further, it had been a boring day, and that it was.

It is important to note that during the time Marcella showed application, dedication and interest in her studies she only saw her father on rare occasions. Her behaviour at home also improved.

By then Marcella was twenty years old and her parents were able to take holidays on their own. She showed responsibility, she looked after the house, Lola, Fluffy her pet pussycats since childhood. She began to show softness and consideration towards them.

She also went on holidays with some old friends from school, and Marcella's parents arranged for them to go skiing and stay at the lodge they were members of, they also encouraged her to go on holidays with other friends and often offered to pay for the week.

Marcella was enthusiastic and more optimistic, less critical of everything; she also demonstrated more affection towards them. Her parents were relieved and happy to see the changes, there was hope that the damage was in the process of being repaired, and with their love and attention things would only get better.

Everything appeared normal until she arranged to see her biological father the day of her birthday.

Her mother questioned Marcella whether it was a wise decision to see him and return once more to the instability she had experienced in the past when she made efforts to contact him. 'He has inflicted so much angst and caused tremendous pain and damage Marcella', her mother told her. 'Do you really think it is worthwhile to put yourself through more anguish?'

She arranged to meet him several days prior to her birthday, when she met him obviously the expectation was that he would have remembered it, after all it was her 21st birthday. To her great disappointment he had forgotten her birthday or pretended not to remember it, when she reminded him it was her birthday, he pretended that she was wrong, and that the correct date was another month and another day.

She returned home furious and told her mother that, it was the last time she saw him and she would never talk to him again.

Her parents didn't organize a party for her, because a previous party had been a true disaster. It appeared to be the custom that the address of a party was passed on, and many uninvited people turned up causing problems related to alcohol.

Marcella, for a long time always made the effort to contact her biological father, but he never showed any interest in her at all, once more the result had been the same, so it was up to her to severe the relationship as she had decided.

There was a ray of hope that her biological father hadn't caused too much emotional damage, or the damage could be repaired with their love, and the stable home they provided for her. They offered Marcella harmony, love and security.

Marcella finished her course, and to give her an incentive to further her studies, they offered to pay for her to continue the design studies in Milan, London or Paris or a city of her choice in Europe; she had to find out about the course she would've liked to pursue, and they would take care of the details related to expenses and accommodation. They hoped that she would've taken the offer, because that would have given her another opportunity to detach herself from her destructive and problematic biological father, and at the same time she would have reconnccted with her dream of being a fashion designer.

To their dismay she didn't show any interest at all. On many occasions they reminded her about finding a course in Europe. Ask at college, they used to tell her. Someone may be able to recommend a course that suits you. All in vain!

Her parents believed that after Marcella made the monumental decision not to see her biological father anymore, she would change for the better, and more harmonious times would follow for her and the family.

Several years before when Marcella had been at her worse behaviour, the counsellor indicated that if children in the situation Marcella was at the time made the decision to get rid of the source of their unhappiness, those children would adjust and become better persons through the sad experience.

Marcella decided to write a letter to her biological father to explain the reasons she wouldn't see him anymore. 'She outlined all the problems he had caused during her childhood; she mentioned that he had spoilt her life with a lot of nonsense and with his lack of interest'. You never paid for my education. You have always been critical of everything, but had never done anything to prove that you have some sort of interest in my wellbeing.

My mother is not a prostitute as you keep telling everybody you meet. I love my pussycats, there aren't useless. I live in a beautiful home, my parents love me. You have caused an incredible amount of disruption to our life with your miserable attitude. I totally agree with the reasons why my mother had to leave you.

I can't bear to see you anymore. I can't talk to you, because you don't listen and you argue all the time. You are argumentative and obnoxious. You think you're always right. I dislike those awful people you call your friends. You live with a horrid, ugly, a ball of lard, uneducated peasant of a woman, and you dare tell me that she is better than my mother, because in your opinion beautiful women like my mother are useless due to their vanity. That is a travesty. I don't have anything in common with you at all, and I don't like you either.

Marcella expected a logical response, or perhaps an apology, or an explanation for his past actions. She did receive a letter which she made available to her mother. It was one page full of absolute bullshit. He blamed her difficult personality for all the problems associated with their relationship; she was a product of a greedy and vain mother, and of course the cause of all the current difficulties.

Obviously she wanted to find some answers, but her letter hadn't achieved anything. Her parents thought that it was very courageous of her to let him know of her decision, and quite likely this event would bring some closure to an unhappy relationship. It didn't eventuate.

The counsellor was wrong; Marcella would turn at times like an angry beast at the most unexpected moment and for no apparent or logical reason. Whatever affected her life at work or in relationships, she without failure would transfer the blame to her parents, almost as if they had made the decisions that had brought her into the situation she found herself, and in a way demanded that they resolve her problems.

The outcome was always the same, and as they told her to take responsibility for her actions that infuriated her to the point that whatever created the situation she found herself in, it became her parents fault, and consequently the argument started followed by the tears and the screams.

Mia and I felt so sorry for all the unnecessary animosity and conflict. Marcella had grown in a privilege background, private education, good holidays, she was introduced to many extra curriculum activities, ballet, theatre, music, tennis, painting, and overall she had love and affection, discipline, and a secure home all her life; like us she was really well looked after.

CHAPTER 8

Our parents decided to go on a short holiday to the tropics, and organized Annette to look after us. Annette has been almost part of the family, she knows of our troubles and sadness because she has frequented our home on a regular basis, and in the past she looked after Lola and Fluffy.

Our parents were emotionally exhausted due to the constant animosity with Marcella, for that reason they decided not to say anything to her, and instructed Annette not to say anything either; if Marcella called, Annette would say that she would let them know she had called. If Marcella asked what she was doing at home, just to say that she was cleaning the house temporarily, because the cleaning lady was on holiday.

Marcella left some messages on her mother's cellular phone, but she didn't return her calls to avoid a possible conflict if she found out they were on holidays, also for the first time they had the opportunity to test the sociologist theory that Marcella planned the arguments and disruptions, and the trigger appeared to be the fact that they would enjoy some time away from her. It was the only theory that could be tested because with an inconclusive result, the real cause of the problem was never found. For a mother it was difficult to believe that her own child would carry on in such a destructive manner.

Our parents had a wonderful holiday. For the first time in twenty five years it was peaceful before departure and peaceful after their return.

The following week after their return, Marcella questioned her mother about the phone calls that had been left unanswered. She said: we didn't have reception at all; that is the reason your calls weren't returned, and then proceeded to let her know that they had been on holiday.

Marcella then asked why she wasn't told.

Her mother answered: 'why did we have to tell you? The fact that you don't live with us doesn't appear to change your pattern of behaviour, and we believed that you would've had time to organize the usual performance that without failure you have always planned for our holidays'.

Marcella's response was to laugh, and she terminated the conversation without saying anything else. That confirmed the sociologist assumption that the episodes were planned, and everything was staged to upset them in whatever way she could. It was a sad reality, extremely difficult to accept.

That, it was, pure and simple, Marcella enjoyed making their life a misery even if it only lasted a couple of days, and she couldn't see it, because she didn't live with them anymore. It was distressing that a person so loved, was cruel towards them.

Did she still expect their marriage to fail? If that was the purpose why was it so? What would it achieve for her?

Marcella's parents have a loving, respectful relationship, they need each other, they love their own company; there is a tremendous affinity and harmony at home. They discuss issues that affect their lives in a logical and civilized manner.

Perhaps there was some envy from Marcella, and her obnoxious behaviour was a way to break up the harmony that appeared too strong for her to accept. On the other hand she was part of that harmonious life, but she didn't want it for reasons unknown to us.

She could've learnt that the antagonistic relationship she had with her biological father was abnormal, and therefore, she should've paid attention, and observe a different relationship which was based on mutual respect and love, and in that way achieve some positive conclusions that would've been beneficial for her emotional wellbeing.

At the time, Marcella told them the story that she had seen her biological father and his horrid wife in the city business district, the description she offered was rather provocative. It was impossible to tell whether her intention was to extract a negative reaction from them, or whether she wanted them to agree with her.

The encounter was in the middle of the week, she saw a couple approaching her, the couple was arguing and looked extremely unhappy; he was walking ahead of the grossly obese, ugly, and un-groomed woman, and she followed some steps back dragging her feet. It was the expression of misery on their faces that called her attention, and she thought what a horribly, unhappy couple. Not very attractive, both overweight, the woman dressed in the most unflattering, teal colour, cheap, tracksuit pants and matching top which made her look plumper than the man.

As they approached, she realized he was her biological father accompanied by his wife. They didn't recognize her, and as they passed side by side, Marcella turned her face in the opposite direction to avoid being recognized, and the possibility of any exchange of words, because she felt embarrassed and disgusted. She thought they were horrible human specimens; that was her description.

On the other hand she said: 'you are so different, you both look intelligent, always happy, well groomed; you both look so well, nice looking, healthy, and I never feel embarrassed by your presence'. It was the only time Marcella ever acknowledged that she, in a way appreciated the parents she had.

After Marcella's honest admission they asked themselves the question. Why does she try so incredibly hard to destroy it?

'There will never be an answer'.

CHAPTER 9

We felines don't understand why humans make such a fuss about certain dates on the calendar, but it seems that life revolves around some predetermined dates.

The end of the year was approaching fast, and our parents asked Marcella if she and Peter wished to join them for Christmas lunch at a little restaurant by the beach. Our parents preferred to spend Christmas day in a simple way without too much fuss; it had been the custom for many years since Marcella's childhood.

Marcella's mother said: 'you should not feel obliged to join us, let me know if you both wish to participate, so I can make the reservation, and there is plenty of time ahead to change your mind if you wish'.

A week later Marcella called to say that they would come and they will be there by 1pm on Christmas day. They also had enough time to change their minds, because the reservation was made four weeks in advance, and if they had any doubt or changed their minds a small penalty would've been paid to the restaurant, or our parents would've shared the table with someone else.

Christmas day arrived, Marcella's parents waited for over an hour for Peter and Marcella to show up. As soon as they sat down and the food began to be brought to the table, it was quite evident that Peter didn't want to be there. He didn't utter a single word apart from the initial greeting.

His eyes were fixed on a wall picture, and he also ogled constantly at a girl sitting at the opposite table. His body language demonstrated that he would've preferred to be elsewhere. As soon as he consumed the food, he pushed the chair away from the table almost indicating that he was ready to get up and leave at any minute. He twisted his body in a way that his head was turned away from Marcella and her parents; after the dessert was brought, he stood up and began to exit the restaurant.

The lunch was a miserable experience. Marcella's parents were taken by surprise by his rude and obnoxious demeanour, as well as the disrespect towards Marcella which they considered appalling, but the biggest surprise was Marcella's acceptance of it.

After lunch, at around 4pm everybody returned home and the presents were opened, Mia and I sensed a rather tense atmosphere, the air could have been cut with a blade of grass. We went upstairs.

Peter sat, examined his present and didn't utter any other word apart from: 'thanks'. Marcella unwrapped her present and asked, 'why she was given that, she didn't want that present'.

They finally left at about 5pm. By the time they left our parents were emotionally exhausted. It was a truly awful day. Perhaps if they had invited an unknown person, or they had sat to share a table with strangers, they would've had a more enjoyable experience.

The following week Marcella called and her mother thought that perhaps there would be an explanation for their odd manner; since Marcella didn't convey any reason for the unpleasant Christmas lunch, she was asked if there was any reason for Peter's rudeness.

Marcella agreed that he had been rather rude, and made the comment that if they thought he was rude, they had to get used to it, because that was his manner towards everybody, basically, they had to put up with it. To justify his rudeness she added that he found them to be too square, rather boring, and he couldn't communicate with them. And she also thought they were dull.

Marcella's parents didn't figure out this was the beginning of the usual argument prior to the holiday they had arranged. The extraordinary performance had begun to take shape, and as usual, it would catch them by surprise.

There were many business activities to be organised prior to a holiday, and multitude of arrangements to be left in place; consequently, they didn't pay enough attention to what Marcella was doing. It didn't make any sense to think that Marcella was planning the biggest disruption she could have ever mastered;

after all, she was living with Peter, so what purpose would it serve?

Her parents thought that perhaps she was angry, because after she returned from her around the world holiday with Peter in May that year, she was asked to stay with him instead of returning to live with them. Surely, by then she would've understood that they had basically reached a saturation point with her bad behaviour, and that by the ripe old age of thirty three if she was willing to spend nine weeks with Peter on a vacation, it was a sure indication that she had decided to live with him, or establish some sort of serious relationship.

Would the uneasiness and the tension she expressed this time, be just simply some sort of revenge for having forced her to make a decision about her life?

The other thought was, that since she had always behaved in such a destructive manner for a reason unknown to them, she had conditioned her psyche to act acrimoniously on every occasion she envisaged there was a possibility, they may enjoy some time away from her.

The same question arose, why? What would she achieve? If she wasn't happy with Peter, she had ample time to tell her parents that she had changed her mind about him; she could have returned home briefly until she sorted out her living arrangements. She was quite capable with her work, and therefore it was possible to have an independent life if she wished.

Once again there was no logical answer to the circumstances our parents were facing. Another thought was that perhaps her anger was such that she didn't even realize what she was doing. 'She is an intelligent girl, they said. She doesn't have a twisted mind that makes her carry on in such a way just to be obnoxious and disruptive'.

'Maybe she dislikes us intensely, or perhaps it is plain hate which is difficult to accept as parents. If it's so, what is the reason for her hate?' What are the perceptions that make her behave in such a conflictive manner.

Her biological father conditioned her at a very early age to develop certain animosity towards them, and to do everything possible to disrupt their life, maybe she is still responding to his programming. However, at the age of thirty three, and in a relationship that appeared to be serious, there was no logical reason to continue a vendetta against them. Whatever caused her perceived problems, made the possibility to find an answer elusive.

On the other hand Marcella's parents were pleased she had finally found someone and although his manner was rather unfriendly, and discourteous, and the age gap wasn't ideal, since he was twenty three years older that her, it appeared that she was happy, therefore, he was accepted into the family, and the lunch was in principal part of that acceptance, but it appeared that Peter had other ideas which didn't match the picture of a happy, relaxed family.

Whether he began to manipulate Marcella to suit his own agenda, or Marcella used Peter to create the upheaval she so much craved for every time her parents organised a holiday, is a question that brings no answer. Doesn't matter how much all of us try to find the reasons, we can't find them.

Marcella's parents had made a reservation for a holiday abroad; they would be away for four weeks from the middle of January to mid February. Marcella and Peter would move to our house to look after us. This was discussed with great clarity since the overseas holiday was booked some months in advance. Marcella instead of expressing that she or Peter didn't want to look after us began to create the usual conflict to make life difficult until the very end.

The cleaning lady didn't want to come to carry out her job while Peter and Marcella resided in the property, she didn't like their manner. Basically, Marcella would've had to do the cleaning and that created an immense obstacle for her; this was debated to the point of exhaustion.

Our parents would leave for their holiday, and therefore, everything had to be resolved in a satisfactory manner for them to be certain that we would be well looked after. They didn't want to leave us at the cat hotel, because throughout our life we had long periods at cat hotels, and vet's cages; they didn't want to expose us once more to that situation. They had to think fast, and find a solution that made everybody happy, and at the same time avoided the usual conflict with Marcella.

With barely a couple of weeks left before their departure, Marcella mentioned that she had an interview for a new job which could commence early in the New Year. Our parents discussed it, and found the perfect opportunity to release Marcella from her perceived obligation to look after us, and in this way remove the cause of tension that was increasing as the days passed by.

It was quite fortunate that the osteopath they visited frequently to fix their twisted back, and neck caused by both of us spreading our body across their bed, was the perfect answer. Jodie was lovely. A country girl who used to house sit, and on many occasions had told them that she was house sitting a couple of dogs, pussycats or some birds, while their owners were away.

Jodie was asked, and to their delight she agreed to look after us. Jodie didn't have a car. Our mum gave her the keys to her new, small sports car. She was absolutely delighted with the offer.

The next issue was to let Marcella know about the new arrangements, and considering her often aggressive reactions it was a surprise to hear that she didn't care one way of another.

'It is better this way, and since you may get the job in the New Year it will save you a lot of travelling'. Our mum said to Marcella.

The problem was resolved in an amiable manner, no anger, no arguments, no screams, and no aggression; perhaps Marcella had begun to change. The new relationship maybe brought some balance to her life, those were our parent's thoughts, until Marcella called five days before their departure in a rather agitated state to tell her mother that she had been thinking about Peter's rude behaviour during the Christmas lunch, and that she would have to tell him how they felt.

Marcella's mother indicated that it wasn't a matter for them to tell Peter about his offensive and rude manner; after all he was a fifty six year old person who knew exactly what he was doing. It was a subject to be discussed between her and Peter and for them to find a solution to his problem, whatever his problem was.

If the main reason for his rudeness was, as she had said previously, that he found them to be boring, there wasn't anything that could be done about it. Peter didn't posses an impressive intellect, and he wasn't the most engaging person either; choosing to spend time with him wasn't a priority for them, however, they had accepted him because she had chosen to be with him.

If Peter felt uncomfortable in their presence for whatever reason, whether he felt awkward because they pursued different activities, had a more intellectual approach to life than him, and their field of interests was far wider than dropping names to impress others, that was the way it was, and there wasn't anything to change just to please an individual they hardly knew. In reality, our parents had seen Peter, more or less, half a dozen times, and during those few occasions he had hardly said anything of interest.

Peter had been welcomed into the family, and accepted as he was; a person different to them, but who appeared to make her happy, and that was enough for them to show their acceptance of him; if it wasn't pleasing to him there was nothing else that could be done.

In addition, his plain and premeditated rudeness was a matter of disrespect towards her, as well as them. It was an important matter to resolve, because to continue a relationship without making clear one's own principals, is the base for discord at a later date.

It appeared that Peter had decided that somehow the acceptance of his rude behaviour was expected, in the same way other people, according to her, accepted his discourteous, dismissive manner. If Peter made the conscious choice to be discourteous and rude towards them, they also had a choice. It wouldn't be tolerated.

The angry beast was unleashed and the screams and abuse began in full until Marcella became so irrational, she terminated the conversation as a sign of defiance. Our mum didn't call her back.

Our parents wondered and discussed the reasons for her outburst. Was that the usual argument before a holiday? Or was it more the truth of the matter, that she did see a problem with Peter's rudeness and was not prepared to confront it? As usual the situation became their problem and they had to resolve it for her.

The verbal abuse continued through her phone calls, when Marcella was so incensed with anger that she couldn't stop screaming, and consequently her fury was transformed into a severe criticism for everything her mother had done until then.

Several phone calls took place before the trip, and Marcella always ended up terminating the conversation abruptly with screams of abuse.

The last contact was the day before their departure, when Marcella suggested that Peter would pick them up and take them to the airport. Her mother's response was: 'Why? We don't wish to inconvenience anybody, it is also unnecessary; we will use a taxi service as we always do'.

Marcella then screamed: 'I want you to tell Peter that he was rude to you, and the best opportunity is while he drives you to the airport'.

'How odd to think like that', Marcella's mother responded. 'Why on earth would we want to begin our holiday arguing with a fifty six year old man about his demeanour, when he is fully aware of what he has done? Is this to justify your necessity for an argument?' Marcella's anger was such that she terminated the conversation without saying anything else.

The following day, Marcella left an angry message; she wanted them to leave their itinerary and the date of their return. Her mother ignored the call.

We didn't see Marcella before our parent's departure, although she continued to leave angry messages on her mum's cellular phone, the calls weren't returned. However, our parents responded with text messages with the information of their whereabouts. The reason behind the text messages was in a way to avoid direct contact with Marcella, and not to give her the opportunity to create conflict and disrupt their holiday, and second to keep some communication with her.

Our parents had a good holiday, they returned after four weeks. Jodie looked after us and the house very well. Jodie being a country girl was accustomed to close all doors, and we couldn't sleep on her bed; it was a little lonely, but she was kind and affectionate towards us.

Jodie was a jigsaw puzzle aficionado, she began to put together a large puzzle on the dining table, and after she worked on it for hours, she covered it with a piece of soft fabric; we were so curious about what she was doing that during the day we jumped on the table and tried to lift the cover to check it out; unfortunately, the little pieces moved and she always said: 'guys I told you not to walk on the table, your mum isn't going to like it when I tell her'.

She also loved our mum's new car. We liked Jodie and for that reason waited for her by the garage door when she arrived late.

Marcella and Peter visited the house a couple of times while our parents were away, we ran and hid as soon as we heard their voices, without our parent's protection we felt somehow vulnerable if Marcella decided to take us away; we sensed Marcella's visits weren't to see us at all, but to create problems with Jodie. Fortunately, our parents made Jodie aware about the possibility of an altercation with Marcella, due to the problems we had with her recently.

They mentioned to Jodie that Marcella had been quite obnoxious; it was also possible that she could be aggressive towards her when she discovered her access to our mum's new car. It could be a trigger for an argument; Jodie avoided any friction, very clever girl.

As soon as Marcella and Peter arrived she left promptly, saying that she had to leave to attend to her patients, in that way she didn't give Marcella the opportunity to create conflict.

On our parent's arrival the only contact made with Marcella was on the phone, we didn't see her, but she was prompt to complain about Jodie. The house hadn't been cleaned and everything was in a mess, she had used our mum's car, the pool walls were black and the floor was extremely dirty, it looked like a green soup, and even a dead mouse was floating in it which Peter had to remove.

Our parents were perfectly happy with Jodie, the house was clean, we were well looked after, we were happy and didn't lose any weight. There were problems with the pool, but it wasn't to do with Jodie; due to the multitude of things that had to be arranged before the trip, and the stress that

Marcella's constant arguments created, our parents forgot to organize someone to do the pool cleaning and maintenance while they were away.

We didn't see Marcella at all after our parents arrived home. During the following weeks she called a couple of times to say that she was coming to collect some items she had left, but she never turned up. It was difficult to understand the reason Marcella was so determined to pursue an argument, until she finally called to say that our mum had to telephone Peter to tell him about his bad manners, by now the whole episode was getting very tiresome. It was déjà-vu at its worst!

Our mum had already said whatever was relevant. At that moment there wasn't anything else to add to this dramatic saga and chain of events. Marcella said again she was coming home to collect some items and wanted to know if everybody was going to be home.

'No, our mum said. We are going out, but you can collect your items whenever you like'.

'No, you have to be there, I want you to tell Peter that he was rude to you'. Marcella responded.

That was the last straw for our mum. She said to Marcella that if Peter was such a wimp and didn't have the guts to apologize for his rudeness, she didn't want to see him for a long while; she was fed up with his spineless manner as well as her aggressive behaviour. 'Next time when you bother to call, talk to me about something of interest, I don't have time to plot and manipulate other people. Find a worthwhile cause to use your time, and energy, utilize the free moments you have to improve yourself, do some meditation, instead of being consumed by petty, useless situations that you have created to spoil your life and ours'.

Marcella's usual scream and abuse followed, and once more that uncontained, ferocious anger surfaced, before she terminated the conversation abruptly.

Some weeks after this incident our mum began to feel sick again; she was afflicted by the same chest infection she had experienced the previous year. This time it was much worse, because the antibiotics didn't work at all. Three months and she still experienced chest pain and fever; some nights she woke up in a lather of sweat. All of us were very worried. She continued with her work, but we could see how hard it was for her.

Our mum made the little blankets of a soft and furry fabric with a leopard spot print, the colour blended very well with the polished concrete floor; in the middle and sandwiched in between the furry fabric, a soft, insulating material that makes the blankets quite comfortable to sit on.

I love my little blankets in front of the window, our mum has placed them in strategic positions, where I am able to move from window to window while I follow the sun's curve; I am a real sun lover puss from a young age, and my nose always shows a bronzed complexion.

Mia doesn't sit in the sun, her thick, black coat makes her feel very hot in a few minutes, and her nose turns hot pink, so the blankets are my domain most of the time and I truly enjoy their softness.

Our parents normally sat for a pause from work in the afternoon at around 4 o'clock and they often discussed the situation related to Marcella. How possible all this anguish our mum used to say. She always had a close relationship with us. In spite of her ugly outbursts of anger and aggression, we had managed until now to smooth the differences, and always have been there for her.

It's unbelievable to think that this man has created all this antagonism to keep her away from us, and the possible influence we may have on her. It's like a bad dream they used to say.

Marcella's new friends didn't see her anymore; of course it was always their fault. We didn't see Marcella either and the odd telephone call was abusive and full of anger towards our mum.

It was as if Marcella was consumed by a horrendous dislike and animosity towards our parents, and her way of expressing it was through such monumental anger. She forgot about us and that we also loved her.

It was our mum's birthday and she was still very sick; since February the chest infection re-appeared constantly. It was already six months since she began to take antibiotics and the general practitioner couldn't give her anymore. Her constant cough sounded like the cough of those individuals affected by lung cancer our dad used to say. We were very worried.

Marcella called to say happy birthday, it was early in the morning, about 8 o'clock and it caught her by surprise when our mum answered the telephone, she talked for a brief period of time and noticed the deep chest congestion afflicting our mum, made a comment about it and said goodbye.

It was July already and she was getting worse, her chest cavity was sore to the point that it was difficult to breathe and her whole body ached due to the cough convulsions; she had intense pain across the chest to the back almost as if a blade had gone through her upper body, the neck and jaw bones felt rigid and fixed in one position, the abdomen muscles were tight and painful. She was a wreck, and although the visits to Jodie the osteopath were frequent and she temporarily repaired the problems, the following week presented the same scenario until Jodie suggested that a visit to the Chinese practitioner, who was situated not far from her consulting rooms, could be of some benefit.

She went the same day, and after the initial examination the Chinese practitioner indicated that she had very sick lungs with a lot of fluid; the infection was affecting her liver and kidneys as well, and the antibiotics the general practitioner had given her, had only masked the problems temporarily. The many antibiotics she had consumed, as usual, also had filled her body with very ghastly toxins, all those chemicals accumulated in the liver, and that was the reason the illness recurred after a couple of weeks.

She began the treatment which only made her feel worse for some weeks, as he had warned her; then she had to visit him every two weeks or until the fluid in her lungs dried out. He supplied some herbs which were in small pill form, and they were easy to swallow which was fortunate, because the taste was horrible.

It was August, and as usual our parents were preparing to go to the mountains to ski. Annette once more looked after us and everything was arranged well in advance.

Prior to their departure to the snow fields, our mum was having lunch with a friend when her mobile entered a call from Marcella. She said to her friend: 'I don't know if I should answer this call, I could bet on my life, Marcella's call is to create an argument before we go to the mountains on Friday this week'.

Her friend rightly made the comment, that Marcella didn't have any knowledge they were planning a holiday due to the lack of communication since late June.

She answered the call anyway. Marcella wanted to know the precise day when they would go on holiday.

Our mum said: You haven't spoken to me for the last two months. Why do you want to know the precise day we are going away? It is irrelevant to you when we go away, you don't live with us. Are you preparing the usual argument before we depart?'

She didn't answer, the call terminated abruptly.

It was really incredible that she had to call exactly a couple of days before the usual holiday to the mountains. Her actions had to be premeditated; there wasn't any other explanation for it.

Our parents didn't know if Marcella was preparing to do something to upset them while they were away, there was also the possibility that she might decide to remove us from home, therefore, the situation was discussed with Annette to make her aware of the possibility of an altercation, if Marcella decided to visit our home during their absence.

They thought that perhaps Marcella would take us with her just to get at them. In their eyes we had suffered enough while with Marcella. To prevent further conflict, they decided to change the locks to make sure that she couldn't gain access to the house while they were away, and save Annette and themselves more agony.

At a simple glance it seems a non event situation, but we all have gone through so much with Marcella, that our parents often asked themselves when all this would change.

Once again there was no answer to her erratic and hurtful behaviour. Everything was incredibly illogical and with no real purpose other than to upset every minute of their lives, and in the process her own.

Our life wasn't disturbed anymore thanks to the love we received.

CHAPTER 10

Marcella's obnoxious manner caused a great deal of pain, and anxiety, and the entire family suffered because of it.

Our mum's health, although, it had shown some signs of improvement, still appeared to be a long way from a complete recovery. The cough continued to wake her up at night, however, the chest pain had diminished, and the rest of her aches had almost left her body. The last month of spring brought warm, balmy weather, it was November when she began to feel a little better and she was able to swim again.

Our mum loves swimming; she says that swimming cleans her soul. I used to stretch on my little blanket and watched her going up and down the pool, always reaching the end of the twenty five metres, and then having a rest to restore her energy.

Our mum's health began to improve little by little, once she began to swim the cough dried out, after five months of treatment and several doses of Chinese medicine, the little bitter pills the Chinese practitioner gave her acted almost in a magic way. Her lungs were finally cleared of fluid, and her liver function improved greatly providing her with more energy, and as her health improved, she began to think about the tremendous grief and pain Marcella's behaviour had inflicted throughout the years, and the coincidence with her lung infection.

It had been ten months since the lung infection began to affect her health; although, she was showing a great deal of improvement, she had to be vigilant to avoid a relapse. She saw the Chinese practitioner every three weeks; he assessed her condition and supplied the medicine.

While she rested in between laps, she began to think about the philosophies behind the self improvement books she had avidly collected, and read throughout the years. She thought that through those books it was possible to find an answer and a way to restore her health.

After her work finished in the afternoon, she began to read those books again with the belief that it was possible to find out a solution, and the methods needed to be implemented to allow her grief and pain to move away, and thus restore her physical and emotional health.

Among the books, there was a lovely book she had bought during a breakfast meeting with the author several years before; the book related physical illness with emotional pain. There she found the answer. Her emotional pain had been transferred to her chest and consequently the lungs were affected. The book explained the reasons for it to happen, offered mantras and mental exercises to heal one's emotions.

Many may think that, perhaps it is all hogwash, but she firmly believed in it; she decided to put these theories into practice, and her recovery process commenced.

It was slow, it required tenacity, and discipline to channel positive thoughts to help clear the mind of grief; fairly soon she started to experience a change in her thinking, and with it the health improved as the weeks passed by. The Chinese medicine was also a contributing factor to her recovery.

Christmas arrived, it was already a year since we had seen Marcella, and the last phone call had been in August, the grief and painful emotions were still very much on the surface. We didn't know what to expect or what to do this time.

To avoid an unpleasant situation, and in a way to mitigate the sadness that Marcella's absence brought to all of us, our parents decided to spend Christmas in the mountains, and Annette looked after us during those days. We were fairly familiar with Annette, she spoiled us to bits with toys and biscuits treats; wc wcre also allowed to sleep on her bed.

Marcella didn't cause any disturbance and the end of the year was peaceful. She did leave a message with wishes for a happy New Year. Our mum sent Peter and Marcella a card but no reply was received.

Our parents had planned a trip to Europe to ski in the Dolomites Mountains, and once again Annette was in charge of the house as well as us. They left in mid January and returned in mid February. Finally, they were able to experience another holiday without arguments waiting for them, but the grief related to Marcella was very raw.

We heard from Marcella sometime in March and June when she left messages for our parent's respective birthdays. She never asked about us. Life continued its course, the situation was very painful, because apart from the messages Marcella left for our parent's birthdays we didn't hear from her at all, and another year passed by.

Our life was peaceful, but we were sad, and although, our mum tried to establish some form of communication with Marcella, she didn't find a positive response. The occasional contact always ended up with Marcella screaming abuse, and terminating the conversation abruptly.

Meanwhile, we continued with our routines, Mia and I have a multitude of choices; we may sleep on our little blankets by the window during the day, or make use of the houses Annette purchased for us; each house is shaped like an igloo with a little round opening on one end, the floor is covered with soft blankets, it is dark and magical inside.

At night we spend a great deal of time watching the wild life from the guest bedroom window, every time I see the bush rats I tell Mia that I wish for an opportunity to catch one, and to be able to show her how easy it is to grab them by the throat.

She doesn't believe my stories from the time I was wild, and nobody loved me or looked after me; although, my seniority commands respect from her, Mia's believes that my gentle nature can't be altered, and to that effect, she is a 'petite brute' as our mum normally calls her.

I discovered a rodent inside the house, by the smell of it, I realized it was a junior rodent, my instinct was on alert, and I began to sniff every corner until I determined his location.

The rodent was in our dad's workshop behind the many file boxes; I told our mum that we had a rodent. Before she went out she instructed me to keep vigil, and to tell her where the rodent was on her return. Sure enough, I was downstairs in the workshop when our mum arrived; with an intense gaze I told her were the rodent was, she instructed Mia to keep quiet, meanwhile, I sat in front of the file boxes and when I saw she had a little basket in her hand, I knew exactly what to do. I moved rapidly towards the boxes to force the rodent out, and as it came out of his hiding place, our mum put the basket over it; she took it out of the house and released it in the bush near a big tree.

It must have been rodent season, because the next day we had a new one inside the house; this time Mia was the culprit, she allowed the rodent to get to the third floor where the bedrooms are located.

It was a juvenile mouse, no bigger that the toy mice of many colours we played with; I had my paw over the little creature, and told Mia to exert the necessary pressure needed to immobilize it, she showed her readiness, I let go of it expecting a quick reaction from her, but she just brushed her paw like she used to do with the toy mice; the rodent began to run here, and there, until we saw it running up the stairs to the bedrooms. I was busy trying to catch it, but Mia always eager to try her new skill, allowed it to escape.

We had the juvenile rodent in the house for three days until I finally caught it, took the little chap to the bathroom and placed it in the bathtub, Mia followed, the two of us, and mouse were in the bathtub while I showed Mia the techniques to catch a rodent; our mum heard the rattle and came to the bathroom to inspect, she tried to catch it with the basket, but it ran in front of Mia and finally went under my furry big belly.

'Franc, the mouse is under your tummy' she said. She gently pushed me aside and there it was, the poor little creature, terrified and exhausted.

Our mum was fairly agile with the little basket and she caught it, and once again it was released in the bush away from the house.

As time passed, and since it was impossible to have a civil conversation with Marcella, our mum decided to write a letter. She called Marcella to ask for her new address since we knew they had moved recently, but Marcella refused to give it.

Our mum then said: 'well, if you don't want to give your address give me your email; I would like to send you a letter'.

'I don't want your stupid letters was her response', and without saying anything else terminated the conversation.

It was important to persuade her to understand that a solution had to be found in order to save the relationship. The future didn't look good with this kind of response from Marcella; a letter was the only avenue left to try. Write down everything as it had happened, with the expectation that it would trigger some sort of logical reaction and in the process some kind of resolution could be brought into being.

'This is as difficult as trying to find a solution to the Gaza Strip impasse', our mum used to say.

With no other alternative, the letter had to be sent to the city shop Peter owned. There was never a response from Marcella. In the letter she recalled all the events of the last two years, as well as some events from the past, with the belief that if Marcella read the letter, perhaps it would be the beginning of some sort of sensible, and logical discussion towards finding a solution to the problem, which appeared to have a hold of her emotions, and was destroying the relationship.

One of the points made, was that since Marcella was a child our mum always managed to sort things out after her outbursts of anger, and life returned to normality, not because Marcella apologized or showed some sort of appreciation for her effort in restoring harmony; it was extremely unpleasant to live an existence where continuous arguments were the dominant part of life.

She wrote clearly and precisely that until her involvement with Peter, unfortunately, the same situation recurred at regular intervals; however, since Peter entered her life, it wasn't a matter of dealing only with her aggression and hostility; Peter's obnoxious demeanour was as well a contributing factor in aggravating the problem.

'In the past, I could handle your outbursts of anger, and awful aggression, it is very different nowadays, and I am not able to cope with it anymore, because it is not just dealing with an unpleasant situation which has been created by you; at the moment is a situation created by you and Peter'.

She suggested Marcella to visit a counsellor to seek help, and if her presence was required to let her know, she, from the bottom of her heart wanted this problem to be resolved. In the past I arranged to visit a sociologist, but you didn't like her, and as a consequence the treatment was terminated well before we managed to find the base of the problem. Had we continued the sessions, all these problems would have been resolved, and we wouldn't experience the sadness we are going through today.

Our mum left some messages on her cellular phone as an opening to establish a form of communication, but there was no response. The last message our mum left was about an incident at home. Marcella had given our mum a beautiful handmade glass vase, Mia jumped on the table and walked behind it, made the vase collapse and it broke into tiny pieces. The vase had roses with a sweet perfume and Mia had to smell them. The message asked Marcella if she remembered where she bought the vase so it could be replaced.

After the letter was sent we didn't hear from Marcella and there was no response to the message either.

Well, our mum said to all of us: It appears to be that Marcella doesn't want to know about us anymore. I am closing the door to this terrible pain and I am going to get better, what will evolve from here nobody knows. Let's leave it to life and its unexpected consequences.

CHAPTER 11

Marcella left a phone message whishing us a happy New Year. Our mum sent a text message to acknowledge and thank her for her good wishes, by this time there was no desire to talk to her; the past two years had been truly horrible, like a nightmare, and after such a long and distressing period everybody felt emotionally exhausted and drained; the will to try again and perhaps to be exposed to more of the same didn't appear enticing.

Our parents went to ski again in the Dolomites Mountains, it was a lovely holiday.

By this time our mum had put into practice all the mantras and mind exercises the self help books recommended; her health had improved greatly, emotionally she was stronger as well; by then the emotions were in the process of change. Our mum never felt angry towards Marcella, she wrote her a couple of letters explaining the issues that created the problem, but Marcella never responded.

We always want to take part in everything our parents do, and without failure end up with our nose into boxes, bags, and drawers. Marcella's messy chest of drawers hadn't been touched since she left home, and the wardrobe was full of her things as well.

We began to clean. The drawers were placed on the floor to empty the contents in an orderly manner; as customary we put our paws on every piece of paper, rolled over the photos, and any other material placed on the floor; finally the mess was separated from other documents, then my claw got stuck on an old envelope; our mum removed the envelope from my paw, and it was then when we found a letter written eleven years earlier when Marcella was twenty four years old; at that time she'd already begun to exhibit a more aggressive behaviour towards her parents.

It was after Marcella had decided to move out of the family home, because she was asked to pay board into an account set for her as a means of saving for her future. That was the cause for her anger at the time, so our parents believed.

In the letter to Marcella she was asked to resolve whatever problems she had, and to come to terms with her anger and dreadful manner towards them. Curiously enough, the circumstances they found today were exactly the same as they found eleven years earlier.

In reality, the cause of the current problem wasn't Peter, after all. Perhaps he was a contributing factor, and was the trigger; his discourteous manner towards our parents was just a small part of the whole episode, the anger Marcella demonstrated towards our parents for not accepting his rudeness wasn't the real reason for her adverse behaviour towards them. Maybe, she wanted it to appear to be that way for some odd reason.

The situation was more complex than it appeared to be.

Our parents compared the letters, the one written recently with the one written eleven years earlier, word by word the content was almost identical. Today there was another person involved, and that made resolving the issue far more difficult.

During the previous episode when Marcella decided not to communicate, the reason for her anger was that from the time she had finished college to that date, all she did was to go out every weekend, spend money on clothing and shoes, never helped at home or showed any interest in anything related to the family. In addition, on every occasion a holiday was planned, a problem of great magnitude surfaced, and she didn't even want to look after Fluffy and Lola, her own pets, anymore.

It was then when her parents decided that she needed a bit more discipline, and suggested that a small portion of her weekly wage should be put into an account for her future. She became extremely upset at the suggestion, and decided to move out of home to a most unsuitable place.

Her parents helped with the move, there were twenty plastic bags she brought from her place of work, the ones used to hang garments on the racks. The bags were filled to the brim. It was the amount of garments she had accumulated in a very short period of time. After she moved out, she didn't talk to her parents for several months, and that was the reason which prompted her mother to write the letter.

At the time Marcella didn't respond either.

When the first letter was sent to Marcella, eleven years earlier, and after there was no response from her, a school friend of hers was contacted to find out if Marcella was all right. He told about Marcella contacting him and asking him to reply to her mum's letter which he declined. He thought all the points raised on the letter were quite valid, and it was up to her to resolve the issues which were bothering her.

Under the unhappy circumstances experienced at the time, it was Marcella's mum who reached to her, and tried to smooth the differences of opinion, which in the end Marcella didn't want to discuss; from her parents point of view it was all guess work because she never showed any desire to resolve what instigated her aggressive behaviour in the first instance.

After her mother made contact with her, life returned to normality while she continued to live away from the family; her parents considered it to be a good move for everybody, there were fewer arguments with Marcella. They also had peaceful weekends away. They thought it was possibly for the best to give Marcella space, and time for her emotional development; she needed to be able to be responsible for her own life.

Marcella had many crises during this period, and she always returned with perceived problems for her parents to find a solution; she sort of forgot about her parents, but as soon as she had problems she made sure to call and ask for help.

There were problems with the people she shared the flat with, problems with guys she went out with, problems at work. It was an endless chain of problems. She always complained and whined about everything; the curious part was that whatever afflicted her was never her fault.

The present situation was different from any past events. It was decided that reconciliation just through her mother efforts wasn't going to happen as it had been in the past. Marcella's horribly aggressive manner had been outrageous, hurtful, and abusive to say the least. From that moment, until Marcella demonstrated some kind of reasonable behaviour, or at least apologize for all the aggression, and bad manner towards them, they would remain distant. None of us expected a positive outcome.

The emotional distance continued to increase, and it appeared that Marcella had no interest in restoring any form of relationship. Our parent's continued to discuss the issues that affected all of us, because we loved and missed Marcella.

Well, our mum said one day: It is almost as if Marcella died and we are recovering from our grief; life will continue. The sun will rise tomorrow, and the moon will give light to the darkness of the night. Autumn will arrive and with it the leaves will fall, then spring will bring new growth and everything will bloom once more.

It is very sad indeed that the only daughter we have can be so full of hate and anger towards us. It appears to be that there isn't anything else to do from our part, we must respect the distance she has placed; maybe that is her wish. We should step aside and allow her to live her life.

It had been nearly three years since we heard from Marcella. Our mum was at work. While she waited for the builder to arrive, her cellular phone rang, it was Marcella. She thought that perhaps Marcella had problems, and that was the reason she contacted her after such long silence. It was strange to receive a call from her out of the blue, a bit hesitant she answered and Marcella was initially quite chatty. She talked mainly about Peter's family.

She didn't ask how she was, or about us, she continued to talk about Peter's family and how wonderful they were; talked about her many trips abroad and their life in general.

After all that she asked how we were and then added: 'I am calling to tell you that I am pregnant. What do you think?'

Our mum's response was: 'if it makes you happy that is the most important thing'.

'Oh, so you don't think it is a mistake'.

'Why would I think it's a mistake? You must have discussed it with Peter and decided to proceed with the pregnancy.' There was silence.

Then Marcella said: 'I knew about the pregnancy three months ago, but I decided not to tell you; I did tell Peter's mother as soon as I found out, because she is old and frail, and I knew she was going to be happy with the news'.

'That is very good, Marcella'. The builder has arrived and I have to go. I will call you later.

No need to call me, maybe we could meet for lunch next week, Marcella suggested.

'Yes, I have to check my diary and I will let you know'.

The following week Marcella and her mother met for the first time in three years. Marcella organized to meet at a department store coffee shop where they could have lunch, and later go shopping; Marcella was talkative and looked well. Her mum was subdued and not knowing what to expect, she didn't say much. From time to time Marcella asked if they had done anything interesting and that was all. She did ask how we were.

Marcella appeared to want her to buy baby items, which she did. She also suggested to Marcella that it was possible to buy some lovely items, a handmade blanket in a store somewhere else where their specialty was accessories for newly born babies.

They met again some weeks later to go shopping, and Marcella seemed to be happy that her mother bought several items for the baby; they didn't have the correct address for the special baby shop where the handmade blanket was sold. It was arranged that she would look for it and buy it next time when she was in the area. Marcella phoned from time to time to ask about details of her mum's pregnancy, how it had been and so forth. Every time she called she wanted to know when she was going to buy the blanket and the other items she had offered.

Well, Marcella, the baby will arrive in April and it is October; I am very busy at the moment, when I find the time I will buy those items as I said.

'I will meet you, if you like'.

'No, Marcella I will do it in my own time'.

Marcella's mother bought the blanket and some other pretty little baby things, then called to let her know that she would place everything in the boot of the car, and would call during the following days to arrange the time she could come to deliver the presents for the baby.

She called Marcella and arranged to meet. 'Meet me, around the corner from where we used to live. I will wait for you by the entry door'. Marcella said.

Why don't you give me the new address instead, so you don't have to wait in the street, it gives me a little more freedom with time in case I get caught with work.

'No I don't want to give you the address. I'll wait for you on the ground floor', she insisted.

Marcella was waiting for her on the ground floor by the building main entry door; showed her the entry to the car park and from there they took the lift to the floor where they lived. The presents were opened, and after Marcella saw the good items her mother had brought, she began to complain about Peter's sister and the rubbish she had received from her.

Everything was in a old cupboard box; cheap, stained and worn out items of clothing to fit a two year old child; that was Peter's sister present for Marcella's baby.

'Well, if you are displeased with the present, dispose of it or send it back. Why do you hesitate to act?'

Oh, Marcella said: 'it will upset Peter's mother who is quite old and frail'.

'Surely you know what to do. Don't complain to me about his family. I didn't come here to listen to that'.

The visit was short and Marcella appeared pleased with the items her mother brought for the baby. Our mum left and from that day there was no contact with her until the day before the birth. Marcella phoned to tell about the contractions.

She went to hospital and called from there, her labour lasted long into the night; her mum called the hospital for the updates until it was around 10pm when the baby was born. Our mum said to Marcella that is was too late to visit her especially, after a long day of labour. She would visit the next day. Marcella was elated with the birth of her child, and insisted that she could come to see the baby at that time. Meanwhile, Peter clearly said to Marcella, and raised his voice enough for her mother to hear, 'no, we don't want them here'.

The following day she brought Marcella a beautiful bunch of roses of several shades of reds and pinks, the roses had exquisite perfume. On the way to the hospital a couple stopped her on the street to ask where she had bought such stunning roses; they also made the comment that roses so beautiful were only given to a person very much loved.

It is for my daughter, she gave birth to her first baby last night, was her answer.

She arrived at the hospital and had a brief conversation with Marcella before Peter arrived. She said to Peter: how do you feel Peter, are you happy? Your wish had been fulfilled.

He responded: 'good'. That was the end of the conversation.

Marcella told her that the baby would be given two names, hers and Peter's mother. Our mum's made the observation that if they found another two names, she could choose later on in life in the same way as she did with her four names, she had selected the one she liked the most.

She told them that they would visit her the next day. Marcella's parents arrived at the hospital at approximately 3pm. Peter stood by the door, and as they entered the room, he was congratulated. There, standing with Peter, was a couple and their two children who were introduced.

Marcella's parents entered the room and greeted Marcella and the baby; they stood against the window and tried to be civil with small talk to the couple, and their children in an already tense atmosphere. Peter didn't say a word to them, most of his conversation was addressed to his friend who was standing by the door. It gave Peter the opportunity to turn his back on Marcella's parents, and ignored them completely.

Marcella didn't talk at all to her parents either; another person arrived and that provided them with the opportunity to leave.

Being ignored isn't a pleasant feeling and since the mood was tense, it was better to depart sooner than to wait until an unpleasant moment developed.

I will see you tomorrow, said her mum and they left.

The following day, Sunday, Marcella's mum arrived at hospital in the afternoon at around 3 o'clock. Marcella appeared to be in a foul mood; as soon as she arrived, Marcella began to give orders to do this or that, and at times said how useless she was.

There were some problems with the feeding and a nurse arrived, and shortly asked her to wait outside while the problem was resolved.

Marcella's mum walked outside the room and while she waited several thoughts entered her mind. Obviously, Marcella didn't want to see her or didn't want her to be there, and probably, it was better to leave; she was about to do so when someone else arrived.

Meanwhile the person who arrived was Peter's elderly aunt. They introduced themselves, shortly after the nurse exited the room, and asked them to move to the waiting area at the end of the corridor, due to the time it would take to resolve the matter at hand.

They sat there, and talked for some time until Marcella and the baby made their way to the waiting room. Marcella was happy to see Peter's aunt and began to talk to her in an animated way, the foul mood she had exhibited some thirty minutes before towards her mother appeared to have vanished, although she continued to ignore her mother's presence.

Marcella was asked if it was possible to take a photo of her and the baby using the roses as a background. The response was as brutal and abrupt as it could be. 'Take the photo here! Take it or leave it, I am not going back to that room', Marcella said to her mother in the same tone of voice she had used previously, when she had arrived at her room.

It was a rather embarrassing situation that she couldn't contain her bad manner and rudeness in front of another person, it was really awful. Marcella's attitude was bad enough while nobody was present, but not to restrain her anger and hate in front of someone else was horrendous.

It was time to leave, she said goodbye to Peter's aunt and to Marcella from the safe distance of the visitor's room threshold.

She left the hospital and went straight home, as soon as she returned and we saw her, we all knew something unpleasant had happened. You will never believe what happened today, and she began to reconstruct the episode that had taken place just one hour earlier.

I don't think after yesterday and today's episodes to visit Marcella is worthwhile; I think it is better to forget about her and her child. We will acknowledge the little girl's birthday and send her a present for that date as well as Christmas. We can't allow Marcella to ruin our lives with her obnoxious behaviour.

It was Marcella's birthday when her mother called her, just over a week after the child's birth. That was the last phone call for a long time.

Marcella did phone approximately two months later, and used a rather aggressive manner, and tone of voice when she asked why there hadn't been any contact with her, and added that they had demonstrated no interest in their granddaughter. Initially nothing much was said with the intent of avoiding further conflict, and since they already had made their mind about the course of action they would take, it was irrelevant to respond to her appalling and insulting manner.

For some strange reason Marcella was very persistent to let her mother know how wonderful Peter's family was, and all the things they did together. There wasn't any opportunity to say much, and consequently, it was better to be silent to keep some peace.

There was another phone call from Marcella when our mum had the opportunity to tell her that it wasn't lack of interest, but rather her obnoxious behaviour, hate, and that outrageous anger, she demonstrated towards them. It created an obstacle which prevented them from seeing her and the baby. Her mother's words didn't make any difference what so ever, Marcella was in such state of agitation and anger that whatever her mother said, was of no consequence to her. Her parents were at fault and that was it. The screams began to fly and she terminated the conversation abruptly.

Four months passed and because of the Impossibility of having a constructive conversation with Marcella, our mum decided to write a letter again. Writing was the only avenue left to express the sentiments that her aggressive and nasty behaviour had achieved.

The letter addressed the same issues that were mentioned in previous letters to her. The new letter was addressed to Marcella and Peter asking them to explain the reason for their totally unacceptable behaviour. One of the most important issues was that if they wanted to have any sort of relationship, they would have to make a significant effort to improve on the current situation, and demonstrate that they were willing to resolve those issues in a civil manner, otherwise there was no point in attempting a reconciliation, and to Peter in particular, it was pointed out that he couldn't argue that the differences of opinion were related to an age gap, since there wasn't any age gap in between them and him.

Once more Marcella was asked for her home address, but she refused to provide the information. We never understood her reasons to withhold their address. Again, the only avenue was to send the letter to Peter's city shop. Our parents expected that perhaps he had some dignity left, and he would reply or at least try to resolve the situation, in case that Marcella hadn't discussed it with him.

There was no response from either of them. Meanwhile Marcella's mum made the letter available to a family friend, a doctor of psychiatry who had first-hand knowledge of the situation. She asked him to give her a professional opinion on the contents of the letter, and whether he thought there would be a chance of re-establishing a relationship with Marcella.

Be brutal if you need to be, she said to him. There is no need to minimize the impact because we believe it is rather difficult turning back from where we are at this point in time. We have stepped back to avoid more confrontation.

His analysis was simple and to the point.

With people like this it is difficult to reason, they tend to blame everybody else for their problems, and as a way out to make themselves feel better, they change the historical events to suit themselves. In general, this type of individual believes that the other party is at fault, it is never their responsibility, and as a norm they do not consider that it is necessary to apologize for their behaviour.

They basically think their actions bear no relevance on the outcome or on the reactions they cause. When I accept a patient with these kinds of problems, I always tell them that it will take a long time for them to get better, and to resolve their perceived problems is a long and arduous journey.

Personally, he added, I don't like to treat people with this sort of behavioural disorder, because it is usually a waste of time. There is no possible solution due to the fact that this type of individual doesn't want to see they are the cause of the problem.

In this case, you have proceeded correctly; you have put into writing something that is very relevant to the future health and harmony of the relationship, but they have to read it, and also have to be prepared to engage in a dialogue where the truth is bound to be painful; it is the only way to resolve the issue.

In my opinion you shouldn't expect a response.

Case closed.

Marcella was contacted once again to find out if they had read the letter. Her response was the same as before. 'I don't like your stupid letters', and terminated the conversation.

After that incident we received a couple of emails with baby photos and we couldn't respond to her emails. Since she didn't want us to have her email address, she used somebody else's email.

Our parents discussed the outcome to the last attempt to find an answer to the impasse; they analysed Marcella's odd and negative response and arrived at the conclusion that perhaps she had planned it that way.

Marcella was twenty four years old when a similar event occurred, and Marcella avoided communicating with them for a reason nobody knew, whatever her parents thought at the time was only speculative, because Marcella never expressed any particular reason for her behaviour.

The relationship only survived due to her mother's efforts to reach out to her, maybe, it had been in her mind that as soon as she perceived that her parents weren't needed, she would walk away from them. That was the only possible answer to the current situation. If this was the case, she must've had a very powerful reason to make this type of decision.

Marcella left a message for our mum's birthday and many other people left messages. She called everybody to give thanks for the lovely thoughts and Marcella was called as well. Our mum left Marcella's call to be the last, because she thought that Marcella's response probably would be unpleasant, and the other people she wanted to thank would notice in her voice that something was wrong since they all knew her well.

Marcella was thanked for her phone call, she then very aggressively suggested that it was time for her to see the baby, and to show some interest, therefore she was prepared to forget and forgive everything. 'You mention the place, the day and we will be there, or you need a psychiatrist to resolve your problems'. She said with tremendous hostility.

Marcella's mother response was: 'I don't respond to aggression. What do you have to forget or forgive? What have we done to deserve the hostility you dish out every time you talk to me?' I have told you many times already, that the obnoxious and hostile manner, your dreadful aggression, prevent us from having a normal relationship, and from seeing you and the baby.

Yes, we would love to see you and the baby when your anger is controlled, or at least you don't express such degree of hostility towards us.

Her response was: 'I don't hate you, I am very angry with you'.

'What are you angry about?' Her mother asked.

'I don't know, was her response', she laughed and once more terminated the conversation abruptly.

Chapter 12

It has been seven years since these episodes began to evolve. Our parents are no longer sad, they finally realized that there isn't any hope of a resolution because as their psychiatrist friend said, Marcella has already twisted the history of events to place the blame on someone else, and therefore she is able to feel better.

She finally accepted that she behaves in an angry manner, and recognizes the fact as she expressed it during the last conversation just before she hung up the phone, but she doesn't know the reason for her anger.

I am only a feline who is loved and pampered, my point of view on this situation perhaps is influenced by the good life I am able to live. However, after listening to all those events I wasn't aware of, as well as the sadness of the outcome, it appeared to be that all the beautiful moments have gone missing, and only the sad memories remain on the surface.

As I expressed previously, this is a story without a happy ending. I wish I could change the outcome. I can only guess that there are so many parents all over the world who find themselves in a similar situation, and yet, they accept their offspring's obnoxious, angry, and demanding behaviour because they know that if something is said, the disputes, antagonism and countless arguments would prevail. They grin and bear it as they say.

Our parents are different. They believe that a relationship of any kind is based on mutual respect and love. If the respect and love are missing the relationship ceases to exist, because the base of it had been removed, it is like a building without its foundations.

The grieving will never end, however, as time passes it will diminish, and soon other emotions will develop. We have already begun to experience the change from the intense pain all of us suffered during the last years. The change is a sort of indifference, and dislocation from Marcella. It has started to emerge as a way to mitigate the sadness an empty relationship brings to the soul, especially when it happens to be a very important relationship.

We still think of her, and our parents continue to talk about her but in a different way, and every time a new and unpleasant episode emerges it confirms once more that our parent's decision has been the correct one. Marcella after all this time and during her infrequent phone calls doesn't show a ray of possibility for a normal relationship. She is abusive most of the time, she screams, she is aggressive, hostile, and angry, because our parents in her opinion don't show interest in her life.

The emotions are as if Marcella existed sometime in the past, but the past is gone, and we all know that time never comes back. There are memories, most of them very sad, the good memories had been erased by time, and those good memories appear to be absent from today's recollections.

At this point in time we don't have the slightest hope of a possible reconciliation with Marcella; that is the saddest emotion to surface, after all these years when opportunities were wasted due to anger and aggression from her part, as well as her hurtful behaviour, when she clearly demonstrated that she didn't want to have a relationship with us, and as a consequence we withdrew to avoid further conflict.

Hope is the last emotion to leave our soul. When hope leaves, everything else is dead.

Let's see what time brings. At present we are content with our life, it is a pity, the situation appeared to have arrived at a point of no return, but life is always unpredictable, and when least expected a new twist appears on the horizon. We have love in our hearts, and firmly believe in the connection we all have with each other.

It is important to show love, even if that love is not wanted, by the fact love is shown there is no bitterness or anger in us. The wound has been very deep and painful, the healing process is well underway, and it would take a tremendous effort to return some of the beautiful emotions from the past, the ones that pain has made us forget.

Life has returned to almost normal, it will never be completely normal without Marcella, she is part of our being and part of our life.

CHAPTER 13

At times we think that we have reached some peace and tranquillity in relation to Marcella, and that after some difficult periods we have achieved some sort of balance in our lives, but it isn't always the case.

As soon as we think that all these horrible episodes with Marcella have finished and there is no possibility for her to invent a new way of causing pain, another chapter begins to evolve.

Marcella's phone calls, although sporadic, are always disturbing, because she doesn't let go of that terrible anger and aggression; it appears to be that she works herself to some sort of state of agitation, and when she reaches a point, she then decides to call already disturbed, and only requires a minor incident to explode and begins to scream.

She normally phones when least expected, and tries to say something about the lack of interest our parents show in relation to her and the baby, who by now would be around four years old.

Marcella times her phone calls almost to the point when she is able to inflict the most pain, and can cause high level of disturbance. One of the many incidents occurred just before our mum's birthday. Marcella already in an agitated mood called to complain again about our parents not making any effort to see their granddaughter.

'Well, Marcella, it isn't matter of interest, everything is related to your horrible, hostile manner and aggression; of course we would love to see you both, but we can't accept your violent and abusive manner. You can choose to be pleasant and civil, but unfortunately you choose the opposite, and we don't respond to aggression'. I said that many times and I say it again.

You have a choice, and for whatever reason you behave in an aggressive and hostile manner; we are also able to exercise our choice and that is to accept or not to accept your hostilities. The silence and distance you receive from us is a product of your choices. Before our mum could say anything else Marcella terminated the conversation abruptly.

It takes time to recover from an episode of this kind. Her tactics are relentless; we believe her to be angry because our parents stop all form of contact with her, since she didn't show any interest in resolving the situation, which in reality was her own creation, the only avenue of choice was to back away and hope that some good sense would prevail.

It was such a simple matter, all she had to do was to ask Peter not to be rude to her parents; it was her basic right. She could've seen us without him if his dislike towards our parents was so intense, and if he couldn't be civil and agreeable for a space of an hour.

She turned this simple matter into a complete catastrophe, and created a level of anxiety which is difficult to understand. The real reason for all this mess we will never comprehend, it is a complicate labyrinth.

A year has passed since the last phone call from Marcella. As a response to her aggression our parents decided that no more presents would be sent to the shop. To try to keep a connection with the granddaughter through a parcel twice a year no longer appeared to be the correct path, since there wasn't any other form of communication.

Out of the blue, more or less after a year, Marcella called to say that she wanted to come home for a visit and she was going to bring the little girl with her.

Many attempts were made until the day the visit finally eventuated. It was a difficult situation because we hadn't seen Marcella for approximately four years, since the child was born. The only communication had occurred through hostile and abusive phone calls. The day arrived and as lovely as it was to see the baby it was also very disappointing. During the short visit Marcella asked when would be the next time our parents intended to go to Paris. The response was that they didn't know.

She then proceeded to tell us that they had been invited to a wedding in Ireland, and they intended to go to Paris on their way, however, the trip was too long for the child, and they weren't sure whether they would eventually go.

How strange, our parents thought, to talk about something so trivial when there were so many issues to discuss.

After we saw Marcella, Mia began to throw up rather frequently; we thought that she was stressed due to Marcella's visit. It was possible that Mia was frightened; she could have felt that Marcella was going to take her away. Mia is a very sensitive pussycat. However, Mia began to do other unusual things like not using the litter box, and leaving her droppings on the bathroom floor, at other times in the bath tub and covering the mess with a towel which she managed to pull from the towel rail.

These incidents happened several times and it was decided to take her to the vet for a check up. Mia had a blood test done, but it didn't show any problems; on her return home her intestine began to protrude and she was taken to the vet again; from there she was sent to the emergency veterinary hospital for an ultrasound and further tests. Once the results were available, Mia had to undergo an emergency operation which saved her life.

Our little Mia spent ten days in hospital. Her recovery was very slow. Our mum had visited the hospital earlier that afternoon, also noticed that Mia was depressed, and even hissed at her when she tried to pat her. The surgeon wasn't available at the time when our mum saw Mia. She left a message for him to call her as soon as possible because she was concerned about Mia's wellbeing.

The surgeon suggested that Mia would recover faster if she was brought home. He said that Mia was terribly unhappy; she growled and hissed at everybody, didn't want to eat and looked depressed.

Our parents left home immediately and collected Mia who was exhausted and looked very unhappy. Her belly's fur had been completely removed, the scar was as long as her stomach, and the effect of the many days on antibiotics was taking its toll. She was weak, didn't want to eat until our mum began to hand feed her with her favourite food. She also started to remove the hospital smell left on her fur with a bit of warm water and a comb; she gently combed her coat until that hospital smell basically disappeared and Mia felt more comfortable.

Three days after her return she was a different pussycat, she began to talk, walk, and as she always did, carried out the usual inspections; she sat in front of her personal heater during most of the day and night, it was winter and without her fur she felt very cold.

Mia returned to hospital after ten days for the post operation check up, and the surgeon was amazed at how well she looked; she was happy and talkative, didn't hiss at the nurses while the bandage was removed. The surgeon explained that half of her small intestine had to be removed because it had a fairly big blockage, and her rectum had collapsed due to the straining while going to the toilet. He didn't think it would present further complications.

Our mum noticed how neat the scar was; she said to the surgeon that he had performed plastic surgery on Mia's tummy. He appreciated her comment.

A text message was sent to Marcella informing her about Mia's condition after the operation. We didn't receive a response.

Towards the end of the year, which would've been six months since her visit, Marcella called to tell us that they had sold their city apartment, and they were renting somewhere. They had the intention of establishing themselves closer to Peter's family who resided in another state.

Our mum never makes comments due to the fact that whatever she may say, it would be misconstrued, and the possibility to be converted into the base of an argument is quite high. Her only response was: 'that's good Marcella, however it doesn't matter to us where you live, because we don't have your address, and that isn't a recent event; it has been for the last seven years'. 'Why are you afraid of giving us your address?'

'I thought you didn't want our address because you always sent the parcels to the shop'.

Was there any point to answer? Our psychiatrist friend was correct; the circumstances and the reasons why everything had arrived at the present situation had been re-arranged to suit Marcella.

Our parents are incredibly tired of Marcella's hostile behaviour because it is disturbing, and after every event our mum becomes ill with stomach aches, nausea, and she wakes up in the middle of the night feeling unwell.

We understand that Marcella doesn't want us to be part of her family and we accept her decision. We wish she understood that there isn't any need to continue with her aggression and hostilities.

Chapter 14

Everything appeared well until I began to feel a bit off colour, my appetite diminished and certain lethargy set in. I was observed for a couple of days and then it was decided I had to be taken to the vet for a check up.

We arrived at the surgery and the vet said I looked normal, however, since my appetite had diminished, it was advisable to have some tests. I had a blood test which indicated some strange enzymes in the liver, therefore, further tests were recommended. I also had an ultrasound, and my beautiful, champagne colour coat was shaven on the abdomen and part of the chest; I didn't look attractive anymore, my luxurious and shiny coat was destroyed, but our mum said that she loved me just the same, and it would be only matter of time before my fur grew again; Mia didn't like my bold patches and hissed at me. She also said I smelt of hospital.

The ultrasound results indicated that there were several abnormalities in the spleen, consequently, I had to have an emergency operation immediately; it was a couple of days after Christmas.

I was operated in early January and like by magic my health was restored. I began to eat the day I was discharged from hospital, however, it was heart breaking for our parents because they had booked a holiday in Europe; they were going skiing, they felt terrible to have to leave just seven days after I was released from hospital. The trip had been booked as early as May.

Although I was well and my energy had returned, still it was a worry for them. Thanks to Annette they were able to enjoy their well deserved holiday. I was in good hands and Annette made everything possible for my recovery. Our mum called Annette every second day to find out about my health, the telephone bill was quite substantial when they returned. Four weeks passed very quickly and they were incredibly happy about my recovery.

Will a feline like me live long enough to see some changes to this sad chain of events? Our lives aren't that long, I am on my 18th year of life, and my destiny has brought me to places and situations I never imagined possible. I've always been grateful for all the goodness that has happened during my life; I have gone from a bad situation, where it was almost impossible to find a way out, to the best experiences anybody could have wished for. I followed my intuition, sometimes I used my wit and persistence to achieve my goals, and my sister Mia was a good ally when I needed one.

That is the reason we are so loved today.

Was it the nice colour of my coat, or was it my haughty personality that helped me to achieve so much, or was it just my destiny as the cleaning lady sometimes says to our mum.

Penny, is the cleaning lady we have for the last two years, she is friendly to Mia and me, she gives us a pat when she arrives in the morning; while she cleans, and we obstinately remain on the spot where she needs to clean, she says that I behave with such aplomb, and style, I must have some royal blood in me, because I am very sure of who I am.

She calls me Francesco, she says that I have a regal personality, she hadn't seen a pussycat in her life able to command the level of attention I attract, and that if I had been born during the Egyptian Pharaoh's reign, she is quite certain, that it would've been my destiny to be placed on a sacred alter to be worshiped by the crowds, who would've left offerings of precious stones, food, and incense at my paws. Such assumptions make my ears blush.

I try not to pay attention to the adulation because I have the love of all my family; I feel their love every day of my life, so does my sister Mia and we return that love tenfold.

There are many lessons to be learnt from this sad story. Bitterness and anger are terrible companions to the heart and soul; those emotions don't justify bad behaviour at all.

Being angry almost to the point of hate is harmful to the body and the spirit; it creates health problems, it clouds decision making abilities, it prevents the mind from receiving the good energies that love brings to the individual, in that way wonderful opportunities are totally missed and wasted.

Being angry, as some religious texts say, is like holding a hot rock in your hand and in the process when someone tries to hurt another, the heat burns one's skin.

Anger and hate are paralysing emotions. The individual afflicted by those emotions is prevented from discovering the answers, which otherwise would present the real cause of the problems that affected life in the first instant; while the process of feeling angry occupies the mind, anger always blames someone else for the unhappiness experienced at any given moment.

I am a feline, and it is easy for us to see these kinds of problems, we felines don't have hate as a strong emotion, we may have dislikes, but humans are different, sometimes humans allow themselves to fall into the anger, and the hate traps, and behave in a way that justifies the emotion; those humans spoil their lives and the ones who are affected by their anger.

The anger emotion which sometimes is transformed into hate is destructive to the point that it creates animosity towards others, when the reasons for all the anger are within each individual who experiences it.

Why to be so angry? The feline world has some sort of etiquette in relation to certain emotions; we walk away from conflict when there isn't a powerful reason for it. The main reason to be aggressive is to protect our territory, and we have ways of marking our patch to avoid intrusions which may create conflict; that is an avoidance mechanism used extensively in the animal world, but humans are different in that respect; they mark they territory with fences and sometimes their fences include emotional barriers such as anger and hate.

Sometimes anger is used as a form of emotional protection, and the anger is based on what happened in the past, or what has been perceived, but the past can't be changed, because time never returns, the only part that returns from the past are the memories, and memories only exist in the mind or in photographs.

In other words anger is directed at the past and the past is allowed to affect today and tomorrow. How worthwhile is it to allow the past to affect the good moments life allows us to enjoy today?

Is it the right path to follow to allow anger to dominate life?

Is it right to allow anger to be transformed into hate a more perverse emotion?

The only solution which appears so clearly in front of me is to walk away, if someone is angry walk away, analyse the reasons for the anger, if there is a real reason to be angry don't argue, walk away, let time heal the wound, give yourself love and send love, and in the process the soul is free of bitterness and life can be appreciated in full. We could call this idea, wise, feline advice, it avoids unhappiness and regrets.

Try, follow it and discover the rewards of a life free of anger and resentment; it doesn't mean that we all like each other to bits. Putting this theory into practice will make life more harmonious and rewarding, it will allow the abundance of life to show itself, and within that great abundance there is joy and happiness. In this instance, it is quite appropriate to remember Julius Caesar's wonderful words, "Tempus Vincit Omnia".

Maybe we could compare life to a rose bush, the branches are full of thorns, however, when a flower blooms the flower's beauty, its perfume and colour make us forget the thorns.

We have a rose bush which gives red roses with an intense perfume, our mum calls our attention when a rose appears, she says: 'Franc, Mia let's smell the new rose'. We walk to the garden, which our mum calls our planet. She lifts us to the height of the rose. We enjoy the perfume, close our eyes, and give her head butts. Meow.

www.ingramcontent.com/pod-product-compliance
Lightning Source LLC
Chambersburg PA
CBHW070953120726
47910CB00004B/1214